**Clarissa found herself high
against a wall with Elias Joss's broad,
hard frame snuggled in against her.
His hand loosely cuffed her neck,
preventing her from speaking.**

"None of what you said has anything to do with
why I turned them down." He lowered his eyes
to watch the rise and set of her bosom against his
wrist. "No contact with you doesn't interest me."

Clarissa blinked rapidly.

Elias watched the changing expressions on her face
as she worked to accept the meaning of his words
and abrupt actions.

"We'll be working together," she said in an attempt
to warn him of imminent drama. Her voice held a
weak, unconvincing tone and she shuddered over
not being able to manage more.

Elias nodded slowly several times then started
kissing Clarissa.

She took the kiss, trying hard not to give anything
in return. The pressure of his tongue testing the
texture of hers was maddening and stirred all sorts
of sensations that she wanted to lose herself in. He
abandoned her tongue to trail his across the ridge
of her teeth. Then, he outlined the shape of her
mouth before starting the kiss all over again.

Books by AlTonya Washington

Harlequin Kimani Romance

A Lover's Pretense
A Lover's Mask
Pride and Consequence
Rival's Desire
Hudson's Crossing
The Doctor's Private Visit
As Good as the First Time
Every Chance I Get
Private Melody
Pleasure After Hours
Texas Love Song
His Texas Touch
Provocative Territory

ALTONYA WASHINGTON

has been a romance novelist for nearly a decade. Her novel *Finding Love Again* won the *RT Book Reviews* Reviewer's Choice Award for Best Multicultural Romance in 2004. She lives in North Carolina and recently received her master's degree in library science. As T. Onyx, AlTonya released her third erotica title *Pleasure's Powerhouse* in 2011. Her latest Harlequin Kimani titles include *Texas Love Song,* first in the Lone Star Seduction series, which was released June 2012. The series title was followed by *His Texas Touch* in July. That year also marked the release of the fourteenth title in her popular Ramsey/Tesano Saga, *A Lover's Sin.*

DISCARD

Provocative
TERRITORY

ALTONYA
WASHINGTON

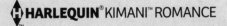

HARLEQUIN® KIMANI™ ROMANCE

To my fabulous readers.
Thanks for letting me do what I do!

Recycling programs
for this product may
not exist in your area.

ISBN-13: 978-0-373-86294-8

PROVOCATIVE TERRITORY

HARLEQUIN®
™ www.Harlequin.com

Printed in U.S.A.

Dear Reader,

Elias and Clarissa's story came in segments. Usually, I'm more settled about how characters will maneuver their way through the story line. That didn't happen here. I was intrigued by the introduction, the meeting between the hero and heroine, first impressions…yet I wasn't altogether settled on how the subplot would parallel the relationship being built. As I continued to write, the characters seemed to dictate their roles. As I allowed Elias and Clarissa to dictate, I was awed by how this story began to flow. I even tweeted about it a month into writing the book! This was a very enjoyable world and story line for me to create. I hope you'll enjoy it as well.

Currently, I'm wearing my T. Onyx hat and working on the sequel to *Ruler of Perfection*.

Find out more about it and other projects by visiting my redesigned website, www.lovealtonya.com. Email me at altonya@lovealtonya.com.

Blessings,

AlTonya

Chapter 1

"I'm on my way…yes, yes. I promise I'll be there soon. What? Yes, yes, Terence was on time." Clarissa David spoke firmly yet softly into her phone's tiny receiver. Glancing toward the front of the town car, she sent a playful wave to the chauffeur who was enjoying a laugh over the conversation.

"You tell Terry not to take any of those back roads he likes to use." The female voice through the phone line was a stern one, but it was laced with a husky undercurrent, which brought a sensual element to the woman's tone.

"Auntie, I promise Terence is running all kinds of lights to get me there."

"You tell him to be careful, you hear?"

Clarissa's lashes settled down over her eyes as she winced, at once regretting the attempt at humor. "I was only teasing. He's being very careful." That time, Clarissa merely shook her head in Terence's direction.

The makings of a frown began to nudge the arch of Clarissa's brows. Of course she was used to her aunt's protective nature but even *this* was a bit much.

"Aunt Jaz, can't you at least give me a hint of what you need to talk about?" Clarissa worked hard to keep the frustration out of her voice.

"No, I can't!" Jazmina Beaumont's clipped phrase was punctuated by a low sigh. "Baby, no, I can't. I'm already taking a chance with having Terry bring you out here to see me about this."

"You know I'm starting to worry, right?" Clarissa's question harbored the same clipped tone Jaz had used earlier.

"Oh, don't do that. I promise you I'm not losin' my last bit of sense just yet but this ain't somethin' I want to talk about over the phone. Now stop asking questions and just get here."

"All right Auntie, all right. Calm down and I'll be there soon."

Jazmina expressed another low sigh. "I love you, baby."

The connection ended before Clarissa could return the sentiment. Regrettably, she didn't have long to mull over the particulars of the conversation. Terence was announcing their arrival just outside Philadelphia, at the stop Clarissa had asked him to make en route to her aunt's home.

"Terry, has Aunt J seemed short-tempered lately?" Clarissa asked absently while tucking her phone back into the beige leather tote she carried.

Terence Egerton laughed, the robust sound filling the car's spacious dark cabin. "You mean more short-tempered than she usually is?"

"Yeah." Clarissa's agreement carried on a gust of abrupt laughter. "She didn't sound quite like herself just now, though."

"Probably the usual mess. Maybe a little more of it." Terence drew to a halt, flashing the high beams to instruct a car facing him to go ahead with its left turn. "You know she's about to start that construction for the remodeling and then she's got them nosy committee people houndin' her about that award," he said.

Clarissa's laughter sounded more genuine. "You sound just like her!"

Terence scrunched his nose. "Now why am I not sure that's a compliment?"

Clarissa continued to laugh.

"So what lucky lady you planning on taking to the Reed House Jazz Supper in November?"

Elias Joss stood working his thumb against his palm in deep circular motions. "Looks like I'll be goin' alone since my date stood me up," he told his tailor.

Stanford Crothers chuckled while taking the measurements of Elias's inseam. "You sound put out over it." His observation carried a teasing element.

Elias couldn't help his grin. "It's not a boost to a man's ego to be stood up by his own mother." He managed to fake an agitated tone.

"Never took you for a mama's boy, kid."

"Stan, I swear, if you keep on rubbin' this in—"

"What? You'll tell her to turn *me* down, too?"

Elias laughed long and loudly with the man who would be escorting his mother to the annual dinner for the organization that benefitted Philadelphia's elderly.

"So has Lilia been talkin' about our date?" Stanford queried. He was seated on a stool where he worked on the cuffs of the trousers. At Eli's laughter rising again, the man gave a slow shake of his head which was covered by a neat salt-and-pepper afro. "So much hate," Stan groaned. "I won't force you to admit your mama's got herself a real catch."

"Whew." Eli feigned relief. "Yeah, Stan, thanks for not makin' me admit that."

"Sure thing, 'cause it's so sad when a younger man has to admit he don't have what it takes."

"I swear." Eli rolled his eyes and pretended to be at his limit with Stan's needling. "Having a suit made just isn't the pampering experience that it once was."

"Aah, kid, there's always the rack," Stan sang.

"Or another tailor," Eli playfully threatened.

"They'd never find the body."

The phone interrupted the laughter between the two men when its ringing emerged from somewhere in the depths of the downtown shop.

"Saved by the bell," Eli cheered.

"Watch those pins," Stan cautioned, pressing his hands to his thighs and pushing himself from the stool. "Be back in a jiff."

Elias stepped down from the raised platform and padded around the room in his socks. Cloth swatches were pinned to the suit pattern adorning his tall, broad frame. Left on his own, he was soon at work with his phone—checking the emails and texts that had come through during the forty-five minutes of the tailoring appointment.

Elias was perusing his missed messages when the sound of humming wafted down from the wrought iron staircase that snaked into Stan's parlor from the sales floor of Crothers's Apparel and Alterations.

At first, Eli only idly listened to the vaguely familiar tune. He was still pretty involved with the phone. As the volume of the humming rose however, his attention veered toward the direction of the sound.

When a dainty pair of tan platform pumps appeared on the landing of the stairwell and Eli caught sight of the legs they were attached to, the phone was forgotten.

Slowly, he strolled closer. Sadly, further insight on the owner of the shapely stems was thwarted by the overhang of the wall.

The humming quieted. "Stan?"

Elias stepped back from the staircase and waited. "Stan?"

Eli heard her call out again, watching as she made her way into the tailoring parlor.

"Stan?"

He heard the soft call once more as she took the last step down. Elias Joss's greenish-blue eyes gazed at the woman who left the stairs as though she were taking a light stroll. Her unhurried steps echoed faintly on the parlor's walnut flooring while she angled her head in an array of poses during her search for the proprietor.

Elias didn't bother to make his presence known. No

doubt she would notice him soon. It had never been easy for him to blend into the shadows, so he had never tried.

Besides, Eli thought, the woman in his line of sight clearly had her mind set on seeking out Stan. Her steps picked up trace amounts of speed and sound as she searched around corners and the tall racks of clothing cluttering the fitting room.

Elias appreciated her preoccupation, for it allowed him the chance to observe her unaware. The phone vibrated once in his hand to signal a new text or email coming through. It was promptly ignored.

Using one word to describe Elias Joss, it would have to have been *workaholic*. Elias smiled at the familiar dig his partners never failed to sing in his presence. They knew him well enough, however, to agree that work always took a backseat when the opportunity arose to conduct an appraisal of the feminine form.

And this one certainly demanded a closer, longer look Elias decided. His uncommon gaze surveyed the abundant curves beneath the provocatively cut dress gloving the woman's Coke-bottle frame. Elias found himself appreciating the day's forecast. The chill of autumn had not yet set in and many were enjoying the unseasonable warmth of the climate.

The dress on Stanford's appealing visitor was appropriate enough for business wear yet Eli surmised that the woman in his midst couldn't have managed *strictly* business wear if she tried. Her body simply would not allow for that.

She wasn't quite short enough to be classed as such. He seriously wondered if the fullness of her ample bottom and bustline would even allow her to shop in the petite section. Elias cleared his throat to mask a softer, more basic sound which was gathering there. Subtle nudges of arousal were beginning to rattle his hormones.

The throat being cleared in the distance caught Clarissa David's ear and she turned suddenly, expecting to find Stanford Crothers. The man who met her gaze instead literally stopped her.

Taking a moment to size him up was the obvious next move. He definitely merited a closer, longer look. It was then that she heard the warning call of her name resounding in her head. The tone was reminiscent of the one Clarissa's aunt used whenever Clarissa had said, done or was contemplating doing something that would make her look like a fool. Besides, she had more important things to take care of than drooling over one of her tailor's clients. She did make a move toward the stranger, though. Perhaps he could help her locate the man in question.

"Hello." Clarissa nodded as she stepped closer and was again stopped by the extraordinary color of the stranger's eyes. The blue-green orbs against the warm, rich caramel color of his complexion was an interesting mix.

Okay this was just unfair, Clarissa issued the silent complaint. How was she *not* supposed to drool over this guy when he was a walking enticement?

Clarissa... The warning tone resumed inside her head. Still, she indulged in a few additional moments of appraising the silent stranger's unquestionably captivating face and broad frame.

"I'm looking for Stanford Crothers," she said eventually. "Is he anywhere around? His staff sent me down." Clarissa pointed toward the ceiling to indicate the main floor of the shop.

She waited a beat before tilting her head a fraction. The stranger was taking his time about answering. Clarissa found herself celebrating the fact that she wasn't the only one having trouble talking.

Elias's silence was due mainly to the fact that he was standing there cursing himself over his rotten luck. The woman with the provocative body had an even more provocative face framed by the chic cut of his dark hair. It was who that exceptional face reminded him of that had him scrutinizing the current state of his misfortune.

Thankfully, Stanford was returning to the cutting room floor. Elias shifted his gaze, barely tilting his head in silent reply to Clarissa's query.

Understandably curious about the stranger's demeanor, Clarissa forced her mind back to her purpose for being there. She looked in the direction the man had glanced and her smile held more than its fair share of relief when she saw Stan.

Stan, equally thrilled to see Clarissa, spread his arms wide. "Sunshine!" he greeted while enveloping her in a bear hug.

"Stan." Clarissa closed her eyes while cherishing the squeeze. "Sorry for just dropping in. I didn't mean to interrupt you with a customer." She glanced toward Elias, who had been observing the exchange between her and Stan.

"Nonsense," Stan balked, leaning back to smile down at Clarissa. "Never an interruption when it's you." His expression changed a bit as his eyes shifted between the two younger people. "Have you two met?" he asked.

Clarissa shook her head. Elias merely looked over at Stan before bringing his gaze again to Clarissa.

"Well, then." Stan took Clarissa's arm and led her over to remedy the situation. "This is Miss Clarissa David."

"David," Elias repeated, a slight surprise holding his rich voice.

Perceptive to a fault, Clarissa's expression took on a knowing element. "Were you expecting a different last name? Perhaps Beaumont?"

"Has anyone ever told you that you look like her? Like Jazmina Beaumont?" Eli questioned in a tone that was half awed and partly accusing.

"Well, Clarissa *should* be the image of the woman!" Stan's bellowing intruded. "She's her aunt."

Elias responded with a lengthy nod as though he were resigning himself to the fact.

"And you are?" Clarissa prompted.

"Sorry, Clarissa, this is Mr. Elias Joss."

It was Clarissa's turn to ease her curiosity. "Are you related to Joss Construction?"

"Started by his daddy back in the seventies." Stanford's information sharing showed no signs of quelling.

Clarissa's dusky brown eyes narrowed a tad as she appeared to be assessing the new detail, but she made no additional comment. Instead, she turned to Stan. "By any chance is my dress ready?"

"Lordy me." Stan laid a hand against the soft salt-and-pepper whiskers that dusted the lower half of his face. "Did I miss a deadline?"

"Oh, no, no, Stan, nothing like that." Clarissa's head shake warded off the man's concerns. "I was on this end for another meeting so I thought I'd stop by and check on it before heading out to Jaz's for a long weekend."

Stan rubbed his whiskers. "Well, there's some stitching that needs to be completed but I expect that'll be done in time for a Tuesday delivery before closing."

"Oh, that's perfect." Clarissa clasped her hands but winced. "Are you sure it won't put you behind with your other clients?" She chanced a look at Elias Joss who still regarded her with unreadable eyes.

Stan threw up a hand to wave dismissively. "You don't even worry your pretty li'l self over that, you hear?"

"Thanks, Stan." Clarissa was beaming once again. "I hate to rush off, but you know how Jaz can get."

"That's one lady who doesn't like to be kept waiting." Stanford chuckled, his kind hazel eyes crinkling at the corners. "I'll have the dress sent to the hotel. You're at the Peabody, right?" he asked, citing the name of the hotel where Clarissa stayed whenever she visited from California.

"You got it." Clarissa moved close to hug Stan again. He gave her a squeeze when she kissed his cheek.

Pulling back from Stan, Clarissa sighed and looked over at Eli. "Nice meeting you, Mr. Joss," she lied in a subdued tone.

"Sweet li'l thing," Stan complimented once Clarissa had gone. "It's a wonder some cat hasn't taken her off the market."

Elias smirked. "Has she ever been *on* the market?" His question was rhetorical. Like most people in Philadelphia, he knew of Jazmina Beaumont as well as her place of business. Until today, he'd never seen or met the woman's niece.

Stanford's laughter came as a huge burst of sound. "Well, if you ask Jaz Beaumont, the answer would be an emphatic 'Hell no!'"

"She's the protective type?"

"That's puttin' it a might subtle, kid." Stan glanced toward the staircase Clarissa had taken up and out of the shop. He shrugged, saying, "Guess it's understandable. In Jaz Beaumont's biz, she's seen all kinds. Makes sense she'd wanna protect her sister's kid from it."

Elias returned to the raised platform where Stan had been taking his measurements. "I wonder if looking so much like her aunt gets her in trouble."

Stan nodded while making note of a measurement on the pad he'd pulled from the burgundy smock he wore. "That answer would be an emphatic 'Hell yeah.' Ain't easy bearing the face of a woman who's been successful at sleepin' with most of the married or attached men in town."

"Guess not..." Elias muttered.

Stan realized the weight of what he'd just said. "Sorry, kid, that was truly crass."

Elias clapped Stan's shoulder. "Crass but true," he said in a reassuring drawl.

Stan nodded and Elias withdrew into his thoughts, wondering if he'd just treated Clarissa David in a less-than-polite manner because of her aunt's history. It was, of course, a history he knew more about than he cared to admit.

"I believe I got everything I need, son," Stan was announcing as he closed his measurements pad.

"So she doesn't live in Philly?" Elias almost didn't recognize his own voice. He cleared his throat and made a pretense of studying his phone while leaving the platform. He put it in the pocket of his walnut-brown jacket when Stan fixed him with a curiously comical look.

"Only off and on when she does business for her aunt." Stan decided not to question Elias's reason for asking. "She has a place out in California somewhere," he added.

"Hard not to be interested in a curvy beauty like that, huh?" Stan finally queried Eli's motives while observing the younger man knowingly.

Eli only shrugged. "So when can I expect my suits?"

"Right." Stan understood and silenced any further questions regarding Clarissa David. "Time frame'll be same as usual, *Mr. Joss*."

Eli grinned. Stan only addressed him as 'Mr. Joss' when he thought his client was being pompous. At any rate, Eli went over to shake hands with the man.

"Have my mother home by midnight," Elias ordered in pretend gruffness.

Laughter rumbled again between the two men. Soon, Stan was clapping Eli's shoulder and telling him that he'd see him around.

Chapter 2

"Now's just as good a time as any," Desmond Wallace kept his voice low as he spoke into phone. "He's humming."

"Right." Desmond had to confirm what he'd just told the person on the other end of the line. "He came in humming. How often does *that* happen?...Right." Desmond ended the call and then headed for his boss's office.

At the door, Desmond applied a soft knock to the wide slab of mahogany and waited.

"Yeah." The quick reply was an invitation.

"What's up, boss? How'd the fitting go?"

"Stan's getting ornery in his old age," Eli said in response to Desmond's cheery greeting.

"Ornery." Desmond laughed over the word when Elias grinned. "That sounds pretty bad."

"Worse than bad. But he's my mom's problem now."

"Oh?" Desmond lifted a bushy brow.

"He's taking her to the Reed House Jazz Supper in three and a half weeks," Eli explained.

"I'm impressed you'd allow that and haven't threatened the man with bodily harm over even looking at Miss Lil," Desmond chided, referencing Eli's mother, Lilia Joss.

"I told him to have her home by midnight. I'd say that signifies progress."

"Indeed," Desmond mused, silently acknowledging that folks often thought twice before they even asked Elias Joss about the weather. For the man to allow someone to date his mother with ease was definite progress for the serious, sometimes unnerving, entrepreneur.

Desmond often marveled over the number of friends Elias Joss could claim. Desmond himself had almost turned tail and run the day he met Elias for a job interview. Desmond would wager he didn't swallow a quarter of the food ordered during their lunch.

Still, somehow Elias had an uncanny knack for drawing people in. He could set them just enough at ease to allow him to determine whether they were worth his time. The technique definitely worked its magic on Desmond, and Eli was pleased enough to take him on as a personal assistant.

Even so, it was no mistake to label Eli as a workaholic loner. While his disconcerting demeanor never tipped the scales completely over to menacing, there was the element of unease he could instill that not many dared to rouse.

"You had a few visitors that weren't on the books,"

Desmond announced, shuffling through the message slips he'd brought into the office. He passed them to Eli. "Maybe we could set some face time with them during the next week. And Mr. Rodriguez and Mr. Brooks are on their way over."

"Crap, what'd I do now?" Elias murmured absently while he scanned the messages that Desmond had taken. His partners Santigo Rodriguez and Linus Brooks had also been his friends since nursery school.

"They have some papers that they need you to take a look at. They've been wanting to schedule some time for a few days now."

"A few days." Eli was still browsing through the messages. "Takes *that* long to make it across the hall, huh?"

Desmond smiled at the sarcasm. The three men each had corner offices on the top floor of the striking black downtown skyscraper.

"They'll need to square away more than a few minutes to talk to you about this," Desmond said.

Harboring his own share of rapt perception, Elias took note of his assistant's tone of voice. "So what's up?" he asked, leaning back in the large gray armchair behind his desk.

"They should really be the ones to talk to you about this, boss."

Rolling his eyes, Eli grimaced at Desmond's stance. This wasn't going to be a conversation he'd enjoy.

"So is this it?" Eli waved the message slips and opted against forcing Desmond to share the reasons for his partner's visit.

"Uh…" Desmond's dreads hid his face when he bowed his head. He looked even less thrilled about sharing the next order of business and appeared as though he'd been delivered when a quick rap fell to the door before it was pushed open a tad wider.

Linus Brooks walked in with Santigo Rodriguez close behind. Elias observed his partners with a mix of curiosity and amusement. The three of them had been friends since before any of them knew how to put together a sentence. As an only child, Eli had considered them the brothers he'd never had.

Santigo Rodriguez wore a smile even when he was fit to be tied out of rage. The trait often proved to be rather disturbing, for one could never truly track Tigo's moves. That aspect of the man's personality proved quite handy though at the negotiating table.

Linus Brooks was almost Tigo's exact opposite. Linus's most distinguishing characteristic had to be his stinging, outspoken nature. The man wore his emotions and opinions on his sleeve, but always made a point of verbalizing them to ensure they were communicated.

The curiosity lurking in Eli's bright gaze gradually gave way to more curiosity. That day may have been the first time in…ever that both men wore twin expressions…of unease.

"Two things," Linus began once the door had closed behind Desmond's hastily departing figure.

Eli rocked back in the gray leather and suede chair behind his beech wood desk and spread his hands urging his partner to continue.

Linus cleared his throat first, saying, "Cleveland Echols is putting his project on hold."

The news nudged some of Eli's curiosity out of the way to make room for confusion. "The framework and foundation have already been laid, right?" He watched his partners display solemn nods of confirmation. "Reason?" Eli spread his hands again.

"Said his investors pulled out." Tigo went to sit on the edge of the desk and toyed with a baseball paperweight that lay there.

"All of 'em?" Elias asked, watching as his partner nodded again.

"Every last one," Tigo added, stroking the light beard shadowing his face.

Eli rocked back in his chair again. "That's crazy... There was all that support for it."

Cleve Echols's charitable endeavors in Philadelphia were well-known. It was the man's more upscale endeavors that earned him a lucrative portfolio and respect in the business world. The financier owned and operated branches of banks throughout Pennsylvania and Delaware. There were even prominent locales in Atlanta, Chicago, Las Vegas, San Francisco and Miami. Echols's plan to construct a new bank was a major bit of news. The latest establishment was to serve as the headquarters for the successful branches.

"So what does this mean for us?" Eli asked.

"Means we come out smellin' good." Linus's wide mouth curved into a satisfied smile but he shrugged. "Not as good as we'd smell with a full project paid for, but our preliminary charge and phase one fees have already been settled so..."

Eli leaned close to his desk and propped his elbows along the edge. "We should keep our ears to the ground about this—see if we can pick up what may have motivated it."

"We're already on it," Tigo said.

"So what's the other thing?" Eli queried after silence dominated the office for several seconds. Amusement returned to his extraordinary stare as it shifted between Tigo and Linus. "Haven't y'all already rehearsed how you're gonna tell me?"

Santigo mussed the wavy crop of hair covering his head. "You won't like it. No matter how we tell you."

"You'd be a fool to put the kibosh on this, considering the Echols's mess," Linus blurted, staying true to his trademark outspoken persona.

"Then let's hear it." Eli smoothed the back of his hand across his goatee.

"We've been offered a remodeling expansion project. Given the scope of the thing…it'd draw on our offices across the country."

Santigo nodded in agreement with Linus's explanation. "It's huge, El. Way bigger than the Echols deal and with the potential to keep us in the black for years."

"More in the black than we already are," Linus included, reading the look on Eli's face.

"Sounds like an offer we shouldn't refuse." Elias reared back in his chair again. "So why don't you think I'll like it?"

"It's not the *offer* we expect you to dislike, but *who* it comes from," Tigo said, then cringed.

Linus stepped over to drop a folder on the desk. Elias leaned closer and brushed his fingers across the label marked with the name Jazzy B's.

Clarissa David stared across the den at the decorative facial tissue dispenser but she didn't trust herself to make the short trip to retrieve one. Instead, she used the backs of her hands to smear away the water that pooled in her large eyes and made a continuous stream down her cheeks.

She'd been sitting immobile for the last ten or twelve minutes. Intermittently, she'd been plagued by bouts of shaking her head in confusion as if some remark had just been made which prompted her disagreement.

No words had been spoken. Clarissa was alone in the room, dazed and in disbelief. Confusion was but one of the emotions filtering her mind at that point. She'd arrived in Media, Pennsylvania, two miles west of downtown Philadelphia in time to have her final conversation with her aunt Jazmina Beaumont. It was hardly a conversation. Clarissa twisted her mouth into what could have been a grimace. The purpose of the gesture, however, was to hold down the sobs crowding her throat. She'd gotten to her aunt's bedside in time for the woman to tell Clarissa only a few things at best. While they were lovely and inspiring, they had barely grazed the surface of all the questions skipping around inside Clarissa's head. Not to mention everything Clarissa herself had wanted to say to the woman who had helped raise her.

Clarissa sat perched on the very edge of an armchair cushion. She resembled a frightened animal ready to take to flight. She was clenching her hands so tightly that they had an ashen appearance. Frustrated by the sight of them, Clarissa hid her almond-brown face in her palms and shuddered.

Soft rubs to her shoulders caused her to jerk upright a few moments later. Clarissa tried and failed to produce a smile for her aunt's oldest friend and business manager, Waymon Cole. Desperately, she reached up to tug on Waymon's hand until he was seated on the arm of her chair.

Clarissa rested her head on the man's thigh as she cried.

"It'll be all right, sugar." Waymon's calm, easy tone was almost as assuring as the manner in which he stroked the wavy, dark hair that tapered at Clarissa's nape into the chic boyish cut that she sported.

In spite of Waymon's words, Clarissa cried harder into his pant leg.

"I just—just talk—talked to he-her." Overwrought, Clarissa barely hiccupped the words. "I came out—out here to see her and—and to talk. I—Terry made a stop. I—I asked him to stop and…" The sobs grew heavier as she bawled. "If I hadn't told him to—to stop, I could, I would have been here before…"

"Shh…stop this now." Waymon brought the firmness back into his voice. "You stop that, you hear? It's no time to sit around blaming yourself." Waymon bent to kiss the top of Clarissa's head. "Jaz wouldn't want that and you know it. Especially not now when you're about to have so much on your plate."

"I don't even—even know what she wanted." Still in the throes of remorse, Clarissa's words sounded somewhat garbled. "She didn't have time to—tell it—tell me anything—I didn't know. I don't know what to do, Way. She didn't have time…"

"Clarissa? Stop. You know that's not true. One thing everybody knew about Jaz was that she never skimped on the chance to tell folks what she expected of them."

Clarissa shook her head against Waymon's thigh before looking up. "I don't mean that." She blinked tears from her red eyes. "She wanted me out here…had something she needed to talk about."

"Something about the club?" Waymon's long attractive face appeared haggard from all the crying he'd done that afternoon.

Clarissa rubbed the back of her hand across her nose. "I don't know, she wouldn't talk about it on the phone. She just said to get out here ASAP." Clarissa buried her face in her hands and shuddered again.

Waymon was back to massaging Clarissa's neck when Jazmina's doctor walked into the den.

"Dr. Raines." Clarissa was on her feet the moment she saw the man.

Steve Raines had been Jazmina Beaumont's physician for years. Speculation ran high that the two had enjoyed more than a doctor-patient relationship. Of course, neither party had ever owned up to the rumor but, when such talk centered around the likes of Jazmina Beaumont, chances were highly in favor of its accuracy.

"How long was she sick?"

"Clarissa." Steve Raines sighed but he had no intentions of providing a sugarcoated response. Jazmina's niece was far more perceptive than Jaz had ever truly realized. "You've always been a smart one," he said.

Clarissa unfortunately was in no mood to be complimented. "How long was she sick?" she repeated, her dusky gaze was like stone and fixed on the handsome fifty-something Jamaican.

"May I at least ask you to sit down?" Steve waved a

hand toward a sofa that matched the armchair Clarissa had just vacated. He nodded when she obliged.

"Jaz never wanted you to worry," Steve began once he was patting Clarissa's hands where she held them clasped on her knees. "She didn't want you feeling that you had to be here full time. She's been having heart problems for years and we—" he pressed his lips together proving how difficult the moment was for him, as well "—we diagnosed her with heart disease. She had a triple bypass three years ago."

Horrified, Clarissa covered her mouth with both hands. Her speechlessness didn't last for long.

"You should have told me!" she lashed out, her eyes shifting in fury between the two men.

Steve was shaking his head. "I couldn't, love. She absolutely forbid it."

Clarissa turned her accusing glare toward Waymon.

"It's true, sugar," he confirmed with the same slow, sad shake of his head. "You know better than we do how protective she was over you."

Clarissa let her head fall as though she had no strength to keep it up. She couldn't refute the truth in Waymon's words. How often had she listened to her aunt advise her, over the last five years especially, to not let the business become her life or even her passion. Remaining true to form, Clarissa had allowed business to become precisely that.

Feeling defeated, Clarissa left the sofa and went to overlook the rose garden Jaz had cherished. Behind her, she could hear Waymon speaking with Steve about the funeral preparations. She turned to rejoin them.

"No. You don't need to sit in for this, baby," Waymon said.

"It's okay, I'm fine." Clarissa's sigh proved otherwise but she maintained. "I need something to stay occupied."

"Occupied?" Waymon mixed laughter with the word. "I promise you'll have more than enough of that. But this is something you should let others handle for you."

"I need to stay busy, Waymon."

"Not now you don't."

She knew the man well enough to know that was the end of it. Deep down—though she'd be hard-pressed to know exactly where—Clarissa knew he was right. Stifling her arguments, she returned to look unseeingly past the bay window.

Elias had been unnervingly silent since Linus dropped the Jazzy B's folder on his desk.

"We've already taken the early meetings," Tigo explained, averting his dark eyes to pull on his shirt cuffs. "We've pretty much done all that we can without your approval."

Eli applied a quick tug to his earlobe and then brushed his fingers along the edge of the legal-sized manila folder. When he'd brought his best friends into his father's business, it was with the understanding that they'd have an equal say in the operations. Unanimous approval was needed before any project was greenlighted.

"The prelim work shows that the project is sound," Linus chimed in. "The pertinent departments have reviewed the various aspects of the deal and everyone's in agreement."

"We can set up new meetings with everyone involved if you'd rather hear it from them," Tigo offered.

"You don't need to do that." Eli's voice was quiet.

"We know, given the history, that you might be hesitant here, man," Linus chimed in again as he expected the worst with good reasons. "If you could just try blocking all that out. Think about the money on the table with another nationwide project in hand...."

Eli looked up from the desk. A smirk triggered the dimples slightly shaded by the goatee he wore. "You've sold me."

Tigo and Linus expelled twin sighs of relief.

"What's the catch?" Linus was first to recover from the easy feelings floating around the room.

"I'll sign on two conditions." Elias reared back again in the desk chair.

Tigo dismissed some of his easy feelings then, as well. "Conditions."

"You two continue to work with Jazmina Beaumont and her people—" he shrugged "—I don't want to find myself spending time with her while this thing's in progress."

Linus and Tigo tried to mimic their partner's shrug. Blatant uncertainty slowed their movements even though working with Jaz and her people was pretty much the manner in which things were going anyway.

"What's the second condition?" Linus asked.

Elias pushed back the Jazzy B's folder across the desktop. "I deal exclusively with Clarissa David."

Chapter 3

"How do you know about her?" Santigo blurted, his easy persona completely vanished. "Why do *you* get the best part of the deal?"

Elias pushed away from his desk, saying, "Because my name's on the door."

"And wouldn't Mr. Evan be rollin' in his grave if he knew *that* was only because you had a lucky night at cards?" Linus accused, his slanting amber eyes appearing thin as slits as they narrowed.

The partners had gone back and forth for weeks about changing the company name. They then went back and forth about what to change the name to. Elias apparently had no allegiance to keeping his family name prominently displayed on the building's masthead. Linus and Tigo were no strangers to the tense relationship Elias shared with his father. Nevertheless, it didn't sit altogether right with them to completely strip away every trace of Evan Joss's existence.

When Eli suggested they settle the matter by a game of poker, Linus and Tigo figured it'd be the only resolution that would be agreed upon. Linus and Santigo often wondered who had been more perturbed when Elias won—them or Elias.

"Clarissa David lives in California, you know?" Linus folded his arms over his chest and moved closer to the desk. "She only comes back here a few times a year to check in on her aunt's East Coast clients. She's not even heavily involved in the construction end..."

"Yet you two have met with her, or am I mistaken?" Eli focused on the bridge he made with his fingers. He knew both men well. They'd have certainly made a point of meeting with Clarissa David during one of the *few* times a year that she visited Philadelphia.

"Is this about business or somethin' more personal?" Tigo challenged, leaning against the desk.

"What difference does it make?" Eli countered.

Playful accusation brought a sparkle to Linus's exotic stare. "You met her, didn't you? 'Course you have." He rolled his eyes.

"When?" Tigo finally moved off the desk.

"How?" Linus tacked on.

By then, Eli was rolling up his sleeves in an attempt to ignore the gradual mounting of his frustration. "When and how I met her is *my* business." His tone was soft, yet cold.

Linus was undaunted. "It's *our* business, El. We can't afford for you to let a personal..."

"Ancient," Tigo interrupted.

"...beef with the woman's aunt to cause us to miss out on this deal," Linus preached.

"I take offense to that." Elias's voice remained low but not quite as chilly. "I already okayed the project. Last thing I'd try to do is sabotage it."

Linus and Santigo couldn't argue the truth of Elias's words. Despite the dramatics that made up their partner's relationship with his father, they knew Eli was of a mind to see the business remain among the top construction companies in the country.

"At least tell us why you want her all to yourself."

Tigo groaned over Linus's question. "Idiot—he just told you that he met her. That's all it'd take."

Elias lost his battle against smiling and shook his head. "I met her while Stan was fitting me for a new suit."

"Humph," Tigo grunted.

Linus nodded and eased his hands into his trouser pockets. "She's a real sweetheart, El—nothin' like what we've heard and what you *know* about her aunt."

"Apple doesn't always fall far," Eli muttered.

"Well, in this case, it fell and rolled right out of the yard," Tigo championed.

"But don't take our words for it." Linus waved his hands. "Could you at least tell us what your plan is?"

Elias laughed. "What the hell, fellas? You think I'd hurt her?"

"I just don't think it'd be good for anyone involved for you to hold Clarissa David responsible for what went down back in the day between your dad and her aunt."

"That's what I'm trying to prevent." Eli's words were genuine. "You guys went behind my back to put this deal together and had the chance to get to know her in the process." He gave a one-shoulder shrug. "I only want the same chance."

Linus and Tigo didn't appear totally convinced. At any rate, they eventually gave their consent with a round of slow nods.

"You wanna keep that?" Linus looked toward the Jazzy B's folder.

"Leave it with Des." Eli massaged the side of his nose. "He'll tell me if there's anything I need to know, and I'll sign whatever crosses my desk."

Left with nothing further to argue, Tigo and Linus slowly retreated from the office. Alone, Elias's relaxed expression was replaced by pensiveness.

"Do you really need to be doing this now? Mr. Cole already told us what happened." Rayelle Keats's round café-au-lait-toned face was a portrait of bewilderment.

Clarissa set aside another one of the folders that was in the tall stack of folders she'd been reviewing, to acquaint herself with the club's most pressing local business concerns. "They should hear this from me." Her manner was a smidge absent.

Rayelle took a deep breath, hoping her "soft touch" didn't fail her then. "I understand what you're saying, Clay," she began, using her pet name for Clarissa. "But nobody expects you to jump mountains today, this week or this month if truth be told." When Clarissa continued to shuffle through the files, Rayelle came over to put her hand over the folders.

"Jaz was like your mother and you just lost her yesterday."

The reminder caused Clarissa's lip to tremble and the folder's contents to cascade to the floor.

"Honey." Rayelle pulled Clarissa up from the desk and into a squeeze.

"I have to be involved in something, *working* on something. If I don't—" she inhaled sharply "—I'll lose my mind. I know I will, Ray."

"I know, honey."

Clarissa pulled back from the embrace. "No, you don't."

Rayelle, a former dancer and choreographer, currently served as manager for the Jazzy B's clubs in the northeast. She was used to dealing with servers and dancers and the stressful situations they often encountered in the profession. Therefore, it was easy for her to detect the chord in Clarissa's voice that had little to do with grief.

"You wanna talk about it, hon?"

Clarissa stooped to collect the papers that had fallen. If there was anyone she could or would talk to, it would have been Rayelle Keats. The woman had started working for Jazmina when she was eighteen. Something had always told Clarissa that Ray's introduction into the world of adult entertainment had come much sooner than that, but Clarissa had never asked. Rayelle always said that her life began when she met Jaz.

Clarissa and her aunt accepted Ray and the circumstances of her life without question. Clarissa had taken an instant liking to the Miami-bred Rayelle, having met her during summer visits. They had been friends for almost twenty years.

"We'll talk." Clarissa nodded when Ray looked over

at her from helping with the papers. Clarissa glanced at the silver watch adorning her wrist. "Later though, after we're done with the girls, okay?"

"You only get to brush me off once," Rayelle warned and then hugged Clarissa over the stack of papers.

Clarissa was slipping on a pair of clogs in time to meet the dancers. Jazmina Beaumont had established her first club in the late sixties. The *seedy* (or less nurturing) side of Philadelphia in those days was where Jaz was born. Who raised her had always been something of a mystery for Clarissa. All she had ever known of her aunt's childhood was that when the Beaumonts picked up their roots and decided to start over out west, young Jazmina had refused to leave.

Clarissa knew that the woman had been on her own since the age of fourteen. How she'd survived was a tale Jaz had never shared with her niece.

Clarissa had a fine idea. Looking into the faces of the young, lovely women who made their living at Jazzy B's Gentlemen's Club, Clarissa guessed a lot of her aunt's history ran parallel to theirs. Clarissa, whose job was akin to recruitment, saw those same hopeful yet guarded women when they were at their most frightened and defeated.

The stories of their upbringings were far removed from fairy tales and romance. Clarissa learned a lot about her aunt through the very girls she gave purpose. In them, she saw her aunt's fears and shame but also the woman's strength and intelligence.

The dancers walked into the expansive room. It had served as Jazmina's office, lounge and private dance studio. The girls arrived in a silent, somber stream.

They all charted a path right to Clarissa for warm hugs and cheek kisses. Once each girl had found a spot to sit in the vibrantly decorated room, Clarissa moved to stand in the clearing.

"By now you've all heard about Jaz's passing. Yes, Meri?" Clarissa pointed to the young woman whose hand was raised.

"Um…we didn't even know she was sick." The petite girl's tone was whisper soft.

A murmur of voices filled the room for a short while before Clarissa raised her hand for silence.

"I talked with her doctor. She'd been taking heart medication for a while and um…" Clarissa cleared her throat when emotion suddenly crowded it. "She didn't want anybody to know, not even me."

Rayelle came over to grip Clarissa's hand. Clarissa welcomed the contact, which gave her the power to keep talking.

"I wanted to meet with you guys to assure everyone that jobs are secure. I've got no intentions of closing down or selling off the clubs." Clarissa gave the news a few seconds to settle.

"I'll never be able to replace my aunt in your eyes and I don't want to. I will strive to give you the same sense of contentment and security you've always felt as employees of Jazmina Beaumont." She managed to laugh although it was clearly shaky.

"I'm, uh, not one for speeches so I'll just end it there. Either Rayelle or I will be in touch with the details about—" Clearing her throat that time did no good. The ball of emotion was wedged deep. She waved off Rayelle, who was moving close to offer more comfort.

"We'll let you know about the funeral service," Clarissa got the words out.

"All right, ladies, that's it for now." Rayelle gave a clap to rouse the young women from their spots on the sofas and settees. "You can head on to rehearsal, makeup or anything else on schedule. We open in three hours."

The girls took time to kiss and embrace Clarissa again on their way out of the office. Rayelle watched until the last dancer had gone.

"You're right," Rayelle said, pulling her hands through her shoulder-length hair and clasped them behind her neck. "I think they *were* better off hearing that from you."

"Hell, Ray." Clarissa leaned against a corner of the white oak desk. "I don't know a damn thing about running a business let alone a strip club."

"Gentlemen's oasis," Rayelle corrected, using Jaz's preferred description.

The words brought a smile and then laughter. The desire to laugh held on to Clarissa far longer than the actual humor the comment merited. It just felt so good to give into the urge.

"You know you're wrong about that," Ray said once they had sobered from the laugh attack. "What do you think you've been doing for Miss J all these years? I can't think of a better person to handle this place."

"I can." Clarissa cast a pointed look toward Ray, who again laughed.

"Oh, no, Miss Clay. I am *not* the one for schmoozing and hobnobbing and grammatically correct speech."

Clarissa's brow rose. "Could've fooled me." She shrugged when Rayelle waved her off.

"I don't know half of what it takes to operate this place." Clarissa glanced at the folders she'd been browsing before the meeting with the dancers. "I don't even know the ins and outs of who might've been giving her problems...nothing...." She knocked a fist against a jean-clad thigh.

Ray laughed one more time. "What are you talkin' about? This place runs like a lean machine. I never heard Miss J complain about any problems."

"Yeah, remember this is the same woman who didn't tell us she had heart disease and bypass surgery, either."

Ray folded her arms at her waist. "What are you getting at, Clay?"

Clarissa spent the next few minutes talking of "the day" when she spoke to Jaz over the phone and how insistent the woman was about talking to her in person.

"That *is* weird, even for Miss J."

"So, in other words you and the girls haven't noticed anything strange. She wasn't acting funny...before?"

"Nothing I can put my finger on." Rayelle's fair features appeared shadowed by worry. "I'll keep an ear open around the girls anyway."

"I don't even know what appointments she needed to keep." Clarissa was staring at the files again. "Only thing I was kept in the loop on was the new construction project. Jaz wanted me on hand to take any necessary trips."

"Guess that's where it pays *not* to be a control freak." Rayelle referenced Jaz's penchant for organizing *all* aspects of her business calendar. Working for Jazmina

Beaumont, a secretary or assistant was left with little to do.

"Know what?" Ray began to leer indulgently. "That's the perfect excuse for dinner out on the town."

Clarissa frowned. "What is?"

"Miss J's appointments. We can go through her planner and get a better idea of her upcoming commitments. I'm pretty sure you won't want to be hanging around here when this place opens in a few hours."

"Mmm…" Clarissa leaned her head back as though she were envisioning the meal. "Add drinks to that offer and you've got a deal."

"Now we're speakin' the same language." Rayelle hurried over to Clarissa. They exchanged kisses and hugs over the stack of folders.

"You threw us for a loop here, sir. We weren't expecting that," Elias told Cleveland Echols when they spoke by phone later that afternoon. Eli had wasted no time asking the man about his decision to back out on the construction of the new bank.

"I am sorry about it, boy, but it's like I told Tigo and Linus. A sudden loss of investors." The man sighed. "Can't say I'm all that surprised given the shaky state of the economy."

"Right," Eli agreed then massaged his eyes. "So that was the logic behind their decision to pull the plug."

There was silence from Cleve Echols's end of the line.

"Mr. Cleve?"

"It's a complex matter, son."

Eli bowed his head then, regretting the strain that came through in the man's voice.

"How long have we known each other, Mr. Cleve?"

Cleveland Echols's soft chuckling came through the line. "Since your mama brought you to the bank to deposit your first twenty dollars." Cleve's laughter continued as he recalled a then seven-year-old Elias Evan Joss refusing to leave his money until Cleve had come out from his office to personally assure him that he'd have access to his funds at all times.

"You should know that I only want to help, sir," Eli cautioned once the laughter had settled. "It should go without saying that you can trust me."

"That's really all I have to tell you, Elias. The investors pulled out and went in with Waymon Cole."

"Cole...how do I know that name?" Eli murmured.

"He's made money for a lot of folks in this town. These days a quality investment banker is a godsend."

"Investment banker—that must be it." Elias didn't sound totally convinced.

"Cole's probably best known though as Jaz Beaumont's business manager," Cleve added after a few more seconds of silence had held the line.

"Right." Elias realized *that* was the connection he sought.

Rayelle decided that her friend could use dinner, drinks *and* a little dress up to brighten the evening. They wangled a last minute reservation to Via!, a restaurant that specialized in hearty grilled foods served in an upscale atmosphere. Jackets were required of all male patrons while female diners frequented the establishment in their sexiest attire.

"Did I do good?" Ray asked as she and Clarissa stood just inside the dining room near the host's stand.

Clarissa smiled brightly and nudged Ray's arm. "Better than good," she said.

The maître d' greeted the women by letting them know how "delicious" they looked. Offering an arm to each, he escorted the ladies into the spacious dining room that blazed golden from the electric candles that were spaced across the area.

Most women who visited the restaurant visited on the arm of a male patron. When two women arrived together as dining partners, the overwhelming population of male customers couldn't help but take notice. This was amplified with respect to Rayelle and Clarissa, who took sexy-chic to another level. The stunning duo drew more than their fair share of attention. Rayelle showed off her dancer's legs in a strapless lavender number. Clarissa's breathtaking curves were gloved in an asymmetrical peach frock that blurred the lines between elegant and erotic.

"Now, how the hell do they expect us to focus on a thing when they dress like that?" Santigo queried, making no effort to mask his delight.

"Guess it depends on what we're supposed to be focusing on," Elias noted, his vivid blue-green gaze locked on Clarissa.

"Who's that with her?" Linus asked.

Tigo shrugged and tossed his napkin to the table. "Guess that means we should go over and introduce ourselves."

"Show some restraint." Elias's advisement was soft. "The woman just lost her aunt."

Santigo stood and dropped several bills to the table as payment for the dinner he had promised his friends. "In that case we should go and pay our respects." His demeanor was serious now.

Eli and Linus rose together and the three made their way across the plush dining area. The partners captured interest in much the same manner that Clarissa and Rayelle had upon their arrival. The male trio had always snagged feminine appreciation quickly and with full awareness. While Tigo and Linus made great use of their attributes, Elias proved to be the more selective member of the group. It was difficult, if it was even possible, for him to put into words what truly intrigued him enough about a woman to pursue her.

Whatever it was, Clarissa David possessed it in droves, and that disturbed him. Elias Joss was not a man who liked to be disturbed.

Rayelle let loose a low wolf whistle when she spotted the sexy threesome heading in their direction. When Clarissa glanced up from her menu, Ray cast a pointed nod in the direction she looked.

Clarissa did a double take when she saw that Elias Joss was part of the group that had garnered such praise. It was unnecessary to say that he had her interested. Whether that was because he was so scrumptious to look at or because he'd reserved a distinctly chilly look for her, she couldn't say.

Nevertheless, a smile did curve her mouth when she saw Santigo Rodriguez and Linus Brooks on either side of Elias. Clarissa pushed her chair away from the table and went to greet them.

Linus was first to take Clarissa's hand and pull her into a hug. "So sorry to hear about Miss Jaz."

"Thanks, Linus." Clarissa patted his jaw when he kissed her cheek.

Tigo moved in next to offer condolences, when he noticed Eli's expression. The look was an effective warning to keep the contact brief. Clearing his throat, Tigo stepped back but kept hold of Clarissa's hand.

"We were very sorry to hear about this. We'd just spoken to her a few days ago." Tigo nodded toward Linus. "She looked like a picture of health."

Clarissa could feel her throat tightening on the now-familiar sensation of emotion crowding it. "She, um... I know she enjoyed working with you both. I hope you won't mind working with me for the duration?"

"Oh, no," Linus said while Tigo shook his head. "That won't be a problem for us, um...Mr. Joss—" he tilted his head in Eli's direction "—has requested to be your go-to person."

Clarissa pivoted on the seductive transparent pumps she wore. "Why the hell would Mr. Joss do that?" she blurted, having forgotten all sense of decorum and politeness.

Santigo bowed his head to hide the grin he feared was about to emerge. Linus covered his mouth and Rayelle hid her face partly behind a menu.

Elias studied Clarissa with a cool look. But for the narrowing of his electric gaze that just hinted at the stirring of his temper, he seemed unfazed. "Will that be a problem for you?" he asked.

"Could be," Clarissa threw back.

Elias allowed more temper to filter his stare. "Then maybe we should discuss it." The words weren't phrased as a request, and he extended a hand which curved around Clarissa's elbow before she could move past him.

"Great," Linus muttered, watching as the tense couple walked away.

Chapter 4

Clarissa began to regret her outburst when she realized Elias Joss wasn't simply pulling her off to the side for a measure of privacy. He was escorting her completely from the dining room.

He seemed to know everyone they passed along the way, which wasn't surprising. Joss Construction had erected an impressive percentage of the buildings in that city. Nationally, their project portfolio was just as impressive.

Clarissa had taken the time to learn more of the business when her aunt first told her of the new renovation endeavors for the club. Elias Joss had been groomed since elementary school to take over his father's brainchild.

So what? Clarissa silently noted that her own business sense was just as noteworthy. If Elias Joss had set his sights on bullying her, he was going to see that it wouldn't be an easy task.

"Let me guess. You own this place?" Clarissa was saying when she stepped inside an empty, understatedly elegant office on the top floor of the establishment.

"I don't." Eli closed the room door. "My company only built it."

"I see," she said as she removed some of the steel from her voice. "So is this what we'll have to look forward to after the construction's done on my aunt's clubs? The head man in charge just taking residence when he feels like it?"

Elias smiled and walked past Clarissa, causing her to turn and follow his move with her eyes.

"We close a lot of deals here." Eli ran his finger along the glass edge of a round red oak conference table. "We bring clients over here for dinner. Sometimes we come up here to handle other things best discussed in more privacy than the dining room offers. There're about eight other rooms like this." He eased a hand into the pocket of the black trousers he wore.

"It's a service the restaurant provides. Your aunt knew about it. I think she had her own office on retainer here." He watched her curiously. "Didn't she tell you?"

Clarissa blinked. "No." She studied the short carpeting beneath her pumps for only a second before locking gazes with Eli again. "There were a lot of things my aunt didn't tell me. Like why you don't—didn't like her or…" She reared back on one leg. "Maybe it's *me* you have an issue with even though I don't know what the hell I could have done to wrinkle your shorts when I didn't even know you existed before yesterday."

Elias took his turn at studying the simple patterns in the carpeting. He felt his mouth twitching on a smile that he didn't want to give. "You think I've got a problem with you?" He began to stroll the room with its soothing burgundy, black and olive color scheme.

"Oh, please, Mr. Joss, that's more than obvious. You act like I stole something off your dinner plate!"

Elias didn't care. He had to laugh then.

Clarissa folded her arms across the draping front of her dress and tried to remain unaffected by the sound, but she couldn't. The deep rumble of the gesture was quite affecting and she couldn't resist giving in to the smile that faintly enhanced the curve of her full lips.

"I'm sorry," Eli managed to say when he recovered from his amusement.

"Sorry?" Clarissa let her arms fall to her sides. "That's an interesting word to get from someone who dislikes you."

Becoming more sober, Eli went to sit on the edge of the table. "You look very much like your aunt," he said next, his striking features shadowed by the dim light provided by the small stout lamp on the conference table.

Clarissa shook her head dazedly and took a step closer to him. "What is it with you about that?" Her wide eyes narrowed noticeably then widened as discovery flooded them. "Did you and my aunt…" She left the inquiry unfinished. The meaning was clear as she indulged in a moment to ogle his provocative face and body.

Elias rolled his eyes. "No," he stonily confirmed.

Clarissa moved closer, saying, "Then…"

"It was my father who she…had something with."

Since she didn't know what to say to that, Clarissa said nothing.

"I only want to know if all you have in common are your looks?"

That admission didn't fare any better with Clarissa and she merely blinked in response.

Elias winced over his word choice, as well. "I apologize for being blunt but you *did* ask."

"Right. So—" she slapped her hands to her sides then "—will your conclusions have you not wanting to work with me on this project?"

Eli shook his head, stating, "I already gave my partners the go-ahead."

"So why request to work with me? Why do *you* care about what kind of person I am?"

Working his thumb against his palm, Eli lowered his gaze to follow the circular moves. "Not sure," he admitted.

That was partially true. He knew that from the brief time they'd spent in the fitting room, she'd infatuated him. He could admit to himself that he wanted to know what she was like in bed. That unnerved him for a different reason given what he knew of Clarissa's heritage. Had the apple fallen far and rolled out of the yard, as Tigo mused, or was she indeed the physical *and* spiritual embodiment of the woman he hated for tearing his family apart?

Clarissa gave a wan smile accepting that an actual answer to her question wouldn't be forthcoming.

"I think we've both got too much going on right now

to put ourselves through more tension and aggravation," she reasoned.

Elias took his time running his eyes over her body. "I hate it that you think it'd be that way."

"Mr. Joss." Clarissa laughed his name. "What else can I think when you can't even stand the sight of me?"

"Oh, I can definitely stand the sight of you." He left the table and walked toward her with a determination that seemed to fuel his steps and his expression.

Clarissa stood her ground. She knew that he was testing her and unfairly keeping his motivations to himself. She acknowledged that it would require a little more effort to persuade him to be frank with her.

"I should take you back," he said once he was standing but a few inches before her.

Clarissa regarded the arm he offered with skepticism.

"I'm not in the habit of biting," he said.

She let him see her smile. "Does that habit apply when you're around someone you can't stand?"

He reciprocated her smile. "Haven't made up my mind yet."

Clarissa kept her gaze locked with his. "So what's in store when you make up your mind?"

Eli's uncommon eyes surged with something dangerously potent. "What would you like to be in store?"

"I'm afraid I haven't spent much time thinking about it."

Eli's smile returned and he observed her hand on his arm. "Let me know when you've thought about it and I'll make every effort to hurry and make up my mind."

"Oooh, I wouldn't want you to rush that."

"Somehow I believe it'll be worth it."

ment. She knew Ray's rough upbringing fueled her words.

Again, Clarissa reached across the gear shift and squeezed her friend's hand.

"Will you at least tell us what you said to her?" Santigo's concern was evident in his voice and dark eyes.

"It's all right, T. We still have the deal." Eli sat on the edge of his desk and toyed with the baseball paperweight.

"If you're looking for a loose woman in her, you won't find one," Tigo promised.

"No." Eli kept his gaze on the paperweight he shifted between his palms. "No, I don't think I will."

Linus dropped a quick knock to the office door and walked inside. "What's up?" he asked.

"Mr. Echols," Eli said.

Linus rolled his eyes while massaging his dimpled chin. "Look, Eli, we both go back a long way with the man, but sooner or later you're gonna have to accept that Mr. Cleve just lost out on a deal."

"Linus is right, man." Tigo sat down on one of the suede armchairs in the office living area. "There's nothing to prove that there was anything criminal about the investors having a change of heart."

"And you two have *no* theories about how Waymon Cole took those investors?"

"El, man, the theory is money and business," Linus drawled on a chuckle. "Sorry but we're just not as suspicious about this as you are." He went to sit on the arm of the chair Tigo occupied. "Mr. Cleve *unfortunately* was just slow to realize that there was blood in the water and his investors were the bait."

Elias left the edge of the desk, slowly massaging his neck and grudgingly, *silently* admitting that his partners were probably right. His spite and disgust for Jazmina Beaumont had him seeing red in all kinds of directions.

He clenched a fist and banged it on his pant leg when he thought of how he'd treated Clarissa the night before. He'd virtually called her promiscuous to her face. It was a miracle that she hadn't hit him.

"El? That it, man?" Linus asked.

Elias threw up a hand without looking at his friends. "I'm done," he said.

When Santigo pulled open the office door, Desmond was right there and looking overjoyed that the meeting had ended so quickly. "Mr. J, you need to contact the Breck Humanitarian Committee. Ask for Leta Fields."

"What's the rush, Des?" Elias took note of the urgency in the man's demeanor. He noticed the grins that Linus and Tigo wore and he frowned. "Des?"

"They need your official response on joining the committee for this year's honoree."

Elias felt a sinking feeling in the pit of his stomach.

Desmond swallowed. "Jazmina Beaumont."

"Sorry, girl," Clarissa was saying to Rayelle when she arrived at Jaz's home that morning for breakfast. They didn't get much business talk done the night before and had made plans to get together that day. "You could've used your key…I just got the coffee out—overslept," Clarissa gushed while waving Ray inside.

"Understandable. That powwow with Eli Joss probably took a lot out of you."

"Don't remind me, Ray." Clarissa was crossing into the softly lit living room. The hem of a beige cotton lounger whipped over the tops of her bare feet. "Bad enough being attracted to a man who hates your guts without having to be reminded of it every day," she said, standing at the credenza to pour out two cups of an almond coffee blend.

"Attracted?" Rayelle stepped out of the coral-colored slippers and wiggled her toes. "I don't think I've ever heard you use that word about a man you've known less than three weeks."

Clarissa shrugged. "So what can I say?"

"Oh, you won't have to justify it." Ray curled up on the cream-colored sofa that faced a long bay window at the rear of the room. "Elias Joss is rich, intelligent, understatedly awesome and sexy as the devil—'nuff said."

Leaving the credenza, Clarissa brought over the coffee. "For someone not good with words, you got quite a vocab." She handed Rayelle a cup.

"Whatever—no changing the subject." Ray waved off the compliment. "Tell me I'm wrong about him."

"You're not wrong." Clarissa gathered up the hem of her lounger and curled on the other side of the sofa with her coffee. "I already said I was attracted to him. The rest goes without saying."

"All right, all right." Ray placed a napkin Clarissa had provided across her thigh and balanced her cup atop it. "I'll cease the nitpicking and just say that I think you've made a perfect choice."

The rim of the cup touched Clarissa's mouth but she

didn't take a sip. "Don't do that, Ray. I'm not making a choice for anything. The guy just caught my eye is all."

"And he's slowly reeling you in."

"Are we gonna use this morning to get any work done?" Clarissa quickly sipped her coffee.

Ray looked to the crate filled with legal-sized hanging file folders that she'd brought over from Jazmina's club office the day before.

"I thought we'd start with the things from her desk and then tackle that bigger cabinet in her office next," Ray said. "That should get us caught up with everything she has in the works."

"The will reading's on the morning before the...funeral." Clarissa sipped more coffee. "Maybe she cut me off completely and I don't even need to know any of that stuff."

"Humph." Ray indulged in a low sip of the fragrant creamy brew. "Everybody knows Miss Jaz was a genius. Smartest thing she ever did was to involve you with the business."

"Thanks, girl." Clarissa nodded. "And thanks for stepping outside your job description to help me with this."

Ray shrugged. "Miss Jaz knew what she was doing when she hired me, too."

Cradling her cup carefully, Clarissa leaned over to draw her friend into a hug.

"You think there might be anything in this stuff about what she wanted to discuss the day she...died?" Clarissa asked the question in her softest voice after she and Rayelle had browsed the files for several moments.

"That depends." Ray scanned a page skeptically. "Do you think what she wanted to discuss was business or personal?"

Clarissa chewed her lip. "Can't be sure… Only thing she'd say on the phone was that she was taking a chance having me come out here to discuss it."

"Mmm…" Ray observed the paperwork dismally. "I can keep my eyes open for anything weird that might pop up in all this, but you might want to start going through her stuff here in the house."

"Yeah…" Clarissa studied the living room's high ceiling, settled for a time on the way the light hit the chandelier above. "It's gotta be done anyway, I guess."

"May be for the best if you do it on your own, but you know I'm here if you need help," Ray offered.

Clarissa smiled and squeezed Rayelle's bare foot closest to her. The two resumed working diligently until the front doorbell buzzed a half hour later.

"Damn…I'm really missing Miss J's house staff right about now." Ray groaned, not wanting to leave her spot on the floor.

Clarissa moved to her knees. "They were all close to my aunt's age anyway. More like companions than employees. Waymon said she made sure they'd be set financially so…"

"Let me get the door, Clay."

"Nah, nah…my butt's fallin' asleep anyway."

"You're not even dressed."

Clarissa was already up and sprinting for the foyer. The hem of the beige lounger whipped about once again. While the garment covered more of her body than it showed, it held greedily to her form in further emphasis of the heart-stopping curves she possessed.

Clarissa was laughing over Ray's reminder. "It's not like I'm naked!" The words rang out just as she pulled open the door to discover Elias Joss.

Chapter 5

"Is my timing bad?" Elias asked while half smiling down at Clarissa.

"I, um…" Clarissa waved a hand in the general direction behind her, trying to find an explanation. She gave up. "Come in." She stepped aside.

Elias obliged slowly. "I don't mind coming back out if you've got company." His stirring gaze made a leisurely appraisal of her attire.

Clarissa raked her fingers through her short crop of hair. "It's not what you're thinking."

Eli appeared as though he'd expected that response. "What do you think I'm thinking?"

"That I'm probably having an orgy to rival anything that my aunt ever did."

Elias's laughter brought Rayelle out of the living room. She greeted him in a demure tone, but her eyes were alight with interest and approval for the man in her line of sight.

"Sorry for interrupting." Ray barely glanced at her watch. "Damn, is that the time? I really need to get going."

"But we haven't even had breakfast," Clarissa said.

"Yeah, Clay, um…" Ray sprinted back to the living room for her shoes, tote and sweater. "I've got things to take care of in the city before the club opens tonight."

Clarissa propped her hands on her hips. "What about the files?"

"Oh, we'll get to 'em." Ray stopped moving long enough to give a proper goodbye. "It was nice seeing you again, Mr. Joss."

"Eli, please."

"Eli," Ray almost gushed.

Clarissa rolled her eyes.

"Clay," Rayelle said before hurrying out the front door.

Elias studied the closed door for a moment. "Didn't think I'd been here long enough to offend anybody," he said.

Hands still on her hips, Clarissa began to tap her fingers there. "I'm sure you know you haven't done that, but you have to know that you surprised me by coming out here. Or was that the plan? Trying to ease your curiosity about me by catching me in the act of… something?"

Elias smiled a broad smile. "So are we going to talk about this in the foyer or will you ask me in?"

Clarissa dropped her hands and simply turned and led the way to the living room.

Elias whistled. "The woman really loved her space."

Clarissa rubbed her hands down the lounger's long sleeves. "Yeah, she did."

Her tone gave Elias pause and he understood that he'd best get to the point. "Your aunt's affair with my dad lasted many years during my parents' marriage. My dad was so...infatuated with her that he wanted to leave us—me and my mom—for her. I was eight, maybe nine."

Clarissa's steely demeanor melted. She walked over to the sofa, sat along the back of it.

"I'm sorry, Elias." Genuine regret pooled in her dusky gaze. "That had to be awful for you at that age." She shrugged her brows. "At *any* age."

"Yeah..." He smoothed a hand across the wavy dark hair tapered at his neck. "But that doesn't give me the right to treat you the way I've been. I really am sorry, Clarissa."

She shook her head and pressed her hands deeper into the sofa. "At least I understand your feelings a lot better now, but you didn't have to make a trip all the way out here to tell me this, you know?"

"That's not the only reason I came out."

Clarissa raised her brows and waited.

"I got a call from Leta Fields this morning."

Clarissa squinted. "Why do I know that name?"

"She's with the Breck Humanitarian Committee."

"Aah...and you're telling me this because...?"

Eli leaned against one of the columns nearest the sofa. "You know your aunt was up for an award." He watched her nod. "They want me to sit on the merit board."

Clarissa's smile held a hint of wickedness. "And did you tell them that you doing that pretty much guarantees she *won't* get the award?"

"I turned them down."

"Should I thank you?"

"I wouldn't." Eli focused on one of his dark loafers peeking out beneath the cuff of his tan pinstriped trousers. "My motives were very selfish."

"How?" She frowned.

Pushing off the column, Eli walked the stunning room. "If your aunt gets the award, they'll want you to accept on her behalf."

"Right…" Clarissa let the word hang, intrigued to know what he was getting at.

"Committee rules state that there's to be no contact between committee members and honorees or the recipients of their awards."

"Right." Clarissa spoke the word that time in a tone of understanding. "But you didn't have to decline sitting on the board. I really do like working with Linus and Tigo."

"Clarissa, that's not it."

"Well, I've had the chance to talk with them a lot, especially when the project was in the very early stages."

"Clarissa—"

"Elias, please, I'm not that fragile. Working together is contact. I understand that. What? Did you think I'd believe you were backing out because my aunt might be the honoree? I mean, I'm pretty sure the possibility has a little to do with your decision, but I don't think you're that petty."

"Thanks." Eli couldn't mask his amusement.

"But it's probably for the best anyway. Last thing we need is for anything improper preventing Aunt Jaz from getting an award she deserves."

Elias was standing near the sofa again and accepting that he wouldn't get more than a word in with Clarissa. He selected another course of action and in one fluid move plucked her off the sofa.

Clarissa found herself set high against a wall with Elias Joss's broad hard frame snuggled in against her. His hand loosely cuffed her neck, an effective deterrent to speaking.

"None of what you said has anything to do with why I turned them down." He lowered his eyes to watch the rise and set of her bosom against his wrist. "No contact with you doesn't interest me."

Clarissa could only blink rapidly and often. Silently, she commanded her lashes to cease moving but it was hopeless.

Elias took great pleasure in watching the emotions change her expression as she worked to accept the meaning of his words and sudden actions.

"We'll be working together."

She tried to warn him of the imminent drama that *contact* and *work* could bring. Her voice held a weak, unconvincing tone and Clarissa shuddered over not being able to manage more.

Elias understood though and nodded slowly once, twice, three times. Seconds later, he was kissing her.

Clarissa took the kiss without giving anything in return. The pressure of his tongue testing the texture of hers was maddening and stirred all sorts of sensations that she wanted to lose herself in. He abandoned her tongue to trail his across the ridge of her teeth. Then, he outlined the shape of her mouth before starting the kiss all over again.

Whimpers escaped Clarissa's mouth as the frenzy of arousal stirred in the most treasured part of her anatomy. He had her immobile against the wall yet her hips writhed minutely as the frenzied stabs of arousal intensified.

Clarissa needn't have worried about slipping. Eli held her fast. His massive frame was snug inside her thighs and sealed effectively and provocatively there. Even so, she kept her hands folded over the biceps straining beneath the cream-colored shirt that hung outside his trousers. She didn't trust her hands to roam elsewhere. Elias didn't have that problem. The position in which he held Clarissa offered him the chance to test the lush portion of thigh and derriere barely covered by a wispy pair of lace panties. The movements of her hips made her bottom nudge his palms in a manner that had him in an almost painfully rigid state inside his pants.

Clarissa smoothed her bare feet up along the crisp material of his pants and wrapped her legs about his waist. The move gave Elias the opportunity to pull her from the wall. The kiss had turned her wetter, hotter. Clarissa was then thoroughly engaged in the act of their mating tongues. She kissed him with a hunger that bordered on desperation.

For a time, Elias simply stood there holding her and kissing her to madness. Clarissa let herself grow heady off the scent of his cologne. She pushed her hands across his broad shoulders, taking great pleasure in the breadth and power that was barely concealed below the surface of his skin. She felt a sound easily resembling a growl vibrate from his chest and through hers. Moments later, he was rounding the sofa and settling her to her back.

Her whimpering was slowly, consistently driving him out of his mind, fueling Elias's hunger that was already peaked at a ravenous level. He kept his weight off her by lying alongside her on the broad sofa. The position left every part of her accessible to his eyes and touch. Of course he played that to his considerable advantage.

Finally, Eli broke the kiss to nibble Clarissa's earlobe. His hands meanwhile tested the appealing fullness of her breasts. She arched her back when his thumb circled a nipple.

Elias raised his head to study her reaction to what he was doing to her. He was stunned by the slash of possessiveness that knifed through him then. He didn't know what to think of this woman's ability to instill such an emotion. Whatever the reason, he decided that it was too heavy a topic to be considered just then anyway.

He dipped his head to replace his thumb with his lips. He applied the lightest suckle with just a bare brush from his tongue to moisten the nipple. When she whimpered yet again and arched more sharply into him, he suckled harder.

Clarissa knew that she should be resisting or at the very least offering a hint of protest. But she didn't want him to misunderstand. She wanted this. Stopping him was out of the question.

Elias used his free hand to span her hip and then thigh. His fingers curled into the material of her lounge dress and slowly he hiked the garment upward. He lost himself in the satin feel of her thighs, which were drenched in a warm color a few shades lighter than his own dark caramel-colored complexion. Elias was at once greedy to feel more. He began to squeeze the fleshy portion that he cupped.

Clarissa wanted more of his kisses and she curved her hands around his neck to draw him closer. Elias groaned while giving her what she craved. His fingertips at the entrance of her sex gave her a start. After all…she was only used to the feel of *her* fingers there.

Clarissa's flinching however was enough to jerk Elias back to the reality of what he was doing. He moved his hand suddenly, as though she'd scorched his skin.

Her brown eyes were question-filled yet trace amounts of understanding filtered in through the confusion. When she bit down on her lip, Elias rolled his eyes and gingerly eased away from her.

Clarissa inched up on the sofa, keeping her eyes downcast.

"Clarissa…" Elias waited until silence held its sway for several uncomfortable moments.

"It's okay. You don't need to say anything."

"But I *should* say something," he argued.

"Such as?" She looked at him then with challenge in her stare.

"I should go."

Clarissa turned away from him. When she heard the front door close, she rested her forehead to her knees.

Barker Grant wore a scowl on what could have easily been classified as a ruggedly handsome face. The scowl however was a permanent fixture. It was one that so effectively darkened his looks that it kept him from showcasing his extensive investigating skills on screen for his employer, WPXI News 4 Philly.

It all mattered little to Barker since he preferred the grit and heat of hunting down leads and uncovering stories that shocked and scandalized. Barker knew that was what kept him alive—alive and happy.

Just then however, the scowl had to do with more than simply the set of his facial muscles. The work board he studied was the catalyst for his current unrest.

"Gotta be a connection somewhere, dammit. *Think, Bar…*"

Elias smiled when he arrived at Barker's office door in time to hear the man's solitary grumble. Another of his friends since the days of diapers and day care, Barker Grant had crafted as respected a name as it was intimidating. People hushed up quick and sure when Barker was in the vicinity. The man could sniff out dirt in the time it took to cover it.

Though Elias had no desire to keep quiet. He needed to talk and he needed his most levelheaded friend to not only listen but to offer up some sage advice.

Barker heard the quick rap on his door and pivoted on the heels of his Chuck Taylors. He grinned at the sight of his old friend. They met in the middle of the office for handshakes and hugs.

"Am I interrupting work?" Elias tilted his head toward the corkboard.

Barker cursed and gave an agitated wave in the general direction of the board. "I could stand a break. What's up?"

"Clarissa David," Elias said, smirking at the mild

frown Barker displayed in return. "Jaz Beaumont's niece."

"Aha…she anything like her aunt?"

Eli grinned. "Not in the way you mean."

That got Barker's attention. He perched on the edge of one of the three desks in his office and waited.

"I don't get the impression that Clarissa's a…"

"Home-wrecking bitch?" Barker supplied and shrugged nonchalantly when Eli told him to have some respect for the dead.

"Anyway." Eli walked the office while smoothing fist against palm. "We're working together on this remodeling project for Jaz's clubs across the country. I'm acting as Clarissa's go-to person for any questions she might have."

"Ha! And whose bright idea was that?"

"Mine."

Barker's smile turned devious. "Guess I should've asked if she *looks* anything like her aunt?"

Elias sighed as though the effort took everything out of him. "God, yes," he admitted.

Barker whistled. "I know the ladies' men weren't too thrilled about giving up the job of seeing to Ms. David's every need." He referred to Santigo and Linus.

Elias and Barker shared long laughter at the expense of their friends.

"I probably should've let 'em keep the job, though." Eli sat on the edge of one of the other desks. "I don't think business will be a priority or even a passing interest for us."

"Well, hell, man, don't sell yourself so short."

"We kissed."

Barker sat still for a while, and then stroked his jaw in consternation. "She come on to you?"

"Not even. She, um…she was just talking and the next thing I know, I've got her up against a wall."

Barker's whistle that time was partnered with a chuckle. "I'm surprised she let you get away with that."

Eli shook his head. "I don't know what I would've done if she'd told me to stop. I couldn't think straight." He spread his hands submissively. "I swear I lost track of time while I was with her, Bar."

"What are you tellin' me, E?"

"It was like—" Eli left the desk "—like she was mine and only mine. I don't know her from Adam and I felt possessive as hell over her."

Barker let slip another lurid curse while observing his friend. "So how are you gonna work with her?"

Eli's laughter was halfhearted at best. "That's what I want you to tell me."

"Man!" Barker doubled over from amusement. "Telling you how to help me with *my* job would be easier."

"I don't doubt it," Eli mumbled and strolled over to the corkboard where he stared blandly for a few seconds until his attention focused.

"What the hell are you workin' on?"

"Somethin' weird."

"Clearly. Is it a secret?"

"Only if you work for WPHY," Barker replied as he cited the name of a rival station.

"So?" Eli fixed the man with an expectant stare.

"Tryin' to see how it all connects." Barker grabbed a tuft of his curly hair and tugged, frustrated.

"Connects?" Eli queried skeptically and turned back

to observe the board again. The space was cluttered with papers, cards, pamphlets and pictures.

The snapshots showcased several properties that Elias recognized as some of the most exclusive areas in the city. Additionally, there were several featuring what appeared to be garden party and charity events. A large circular space was left clear in the middle of the board.

Eli moved closer to peer at the documents clustered among the pictures. He could tell that many of them were tax notices for property owned by some of the city's most notorious characters.

"What are you diggin' into, Bar?"

"I don't know."

"But you know there's something here?" Eli turned to find Barker nodding. He looked back at the board. "What goes in the clear space?"

"The one thing all this crap has in common."

"Which is?"

"More like, *who* is."

Eli waited while Barker moved to rummage around on the desk before retrieving another picture. Barker handed him the photo and Eli's head snapped up a second after he'd scanned the 5x7.

Barker's smile was grim. "That's right. Our friendly neighborhood banker."

Chapter 6

"Cleve Echols?" Eli's tone and expression were incredulous.

"He's the only thing that glues all the pieces."

"Barker, listen, if you think Cleve Echols could—"

"Hold on a minute." Barker raised his hands and winced. "Now look. I was as close to Mr. Cleve as you were. My mother never had money to put in his bank but she made sure we took a trip there every week so I could see that a black man was good for more than shootin' pool and beatin' his wife." Barker took the 5x7 photo and slapped it to his palm.

"That's why I haven't pinned this up there—he's not where the story ends."

"All right." Eli stroked his goatee and shifted his weight. "So you don't have all the pieces and I'm damn well not questioning your nose for dirt, but I gotta ask what the hell got you snoopin' into this?"

Barker tossed aside the photo. "There was word about Mr. Cleve having money problems."

"Bull."

"True. I swear it." Barker looked even more distressed. "I wouldn't be surprised if he didn't back out of that deal you've got in the works with him."

Elias grinned. He knew better than to waste his time asking Barker how he knew about the project.

"Project was scrapped," Eli went ahead and confirmed. "Being broke isn't a crime, Bar."

"I didn't say it was. I'm only telling you why I started snooping."

Eli spread his hands, urging Barker to continue.

"When I heard this rumor, I wanted to help him." Barker ran all ten fingers through his mass of dark hair and studied the corkboard. "Thought I could set him up with some folks who could help—other bankers maybe? In these times, goin' out of business is nothin' new, but I hate to see it happen to good people like Mr. Cleve."

Barker reclaimed his perch on the desk closest to the board. "God knows we've done enough stories lately on this. I've made a ton of contacts because of it, but I couldn't get one of those contacts to touch the man." He shrugged his brows at Eli. "The whole drug dealer clientele and all."

Elias grimaced, recalling that Linus shared the same concerns when Joss Construction had been approached about the project.

"'Alleged' drug money supposedly constitutes upwards of thirty percent of Echols's bank holdings."

"That soft heart of his," Eli groaned the words and began to pace the large office again. "Never turned his back on anybody he thought he could help."

"And that got me to thinking." Barker pointed a finger to the ceiling. "How could the man be having money problems with those kinds of dollars funneling in? I was able to uncover the fact that their deposits had dried up along the same time that their property tax bills came due. Those cats had seen a fifty percent increase in those fees."

Eli whistled. "Hell, that can't be right."

"Right as rain." Barker snatched one of the documents from the board.

"You think Mr. Cleve had somethin' to do with it?"

Barker thumped a finger against the page he'd pulled from the board. "I think all his high-level clients suddenly experienced money problems. These drug guys were just of the highest profile. We've run loads of stories on 'em." He pointed to the photos.

"Those snapshots there, properties all owned by Echols's bank customers, sites of their charity events. *They've* seen maybe a two percent tax hike. Now either somebody's tryin' to take down these folks who just *happen* to be Mr. Cleve's most notorious customers or they were tryin' to take down Mr. Cleve himself."

A phone buzzed and as Barker tried doggedly not to be attached at the hip to his, he knew the sound had emerged from the phone belonging to his workaholic friend.

It wasn't a call but a reminder from Eli's calendar. His expression softened even as he winced over the message.

"Meeting with Clarissa," he shared.

Barker raised one eyebrow. "Twice in one day…"

"First one wasn't scheduled."

"Maybe she'll cancel," Barker mused and grinned at the look Eli sent him. "But that move would only have you heading back out there for a second visit."

"Thanks." Eli's reply was drenched in sarcasm but he still moved close to shake hands with Barker.

"Always happy to help," Barker stated then chuckled.

Clarissa was in the midst of accepting hugs from Waymon Cole's executive staff. Everyone was filled with condolences for Jaz Beaumont. Waymon moved in last to hug. He kept his arm around Clarissa's shoulders while he led her to his office. There, he escorted her into one of the chairs before a wide mahogany desk that claimed an unfair amount of space. The glossy piece of furniture was broad enough to support two desktop computers on either end.

"I'm sorry we had to do this here, sugar." Waymon squeezed Clarissa's shoulders once she was seated. "And…now…" he added a softer tone on the way behind his desk.

Clarissa smiled sadly at Waymon's nonverbal mention of the funeral. He had been her aunt's oldest friend. He had perhaps known the woman better than her own family.

"Had to be done." Somehow Clarissa forced strength into her voice.

"Timing's still poor but with everything I have going on, it's the only time I could make for Martin."

Clarissa glanced around the well-lit office but there was no sign of Jazmina's lawyer, Martin Rath.

"Oh, he'll be along." Waymon read her expression and shifted his tall lean frame in the chair behind the desk. "I wanted some time alone with you. How are you doing, really?"

"Better than I expected." Clarissa set her tote to the matching chair next to hers and crossed her legs. "Keeping busy helps." She cleared her throat when the image flashed of Elias Joss pinning her to the wall earlier that day.

Waymon's expression reflected concern and a hint of doubt. "You need to pace yourself, sugar."

"I'm tryin'." Clarissa slouched a little in a chair. "There's just so much to learn. So much Aunt Jaz didn't tell me—didn't want me to know."

"Such as?" Waymon's sharp features took on a more notable edge.

Clarissa recrossed her legs. "Just something she was trying to tell me that last day." She laced her hands in her lap and inhaled loudly.

"It's important that you take it easy, all right?" Waymon grabbed a pen and twirled it around his fingers. "Chances are that Martin will tell you Jaz left everything in your name. Makes sense, you were her heart." He smiled when she frowned over the advice.

"Don't play the innocent, miss. You work yourself too hard, and I know Jaz hated herself for putting so much on you."

"But she...she didn't." Clarissa suddenly recalled her aunt's last words to her: *be aware, be careful, live... and fall in love.*

"You're about to become a very powerful woman in a very bold business." Waymon ran a hand down the side of his long face. "People are quick to turn up their noses at adult entertainment, yet privately they funnel impressive amounts of money into it. If you think just looking like Jaz has made your life hard, imagine how hard it's about to become now that you'll be heading the business that made your aunt a scandal."

Clarissa studied the hem of her burgundy shirt dress. "Wasn't just the business that did that, Way."

Waymon grimaced over the reference to Jaz's predilection for attached men. With a nod, he acknowledged the truth of it. "I think *that* even had a lot to do with the business. The club left her with little time for crafting a real life—a real relationship. With a married man... she could have the joys of companionship without the work required to make a relationship last."

Clarissa sniffled at the waste of it all.

"I think she finally realized the folly in all that," Waymon said. "After all, there were wives involved... and children."

Again, Clarissa had the image of Eli Joss in her head.

Waymon leaned across his desk. "I only want you to know that no one expects for you to carry on for Jaz. There are plenty here who'd happily oversee things. You remember that."

There was a knock on the office door and then a short, slender Caucasian man with sparkling dark eyes and an approachable smile stepped into the room.

Clarissa laughed the instant she saw him. She had always held a fondness for the playfully formal man.

Out of habit, Martin Rath hastily brushed back the shock of grayish-blond hair that consistently fell across his forehead. The unmanageable locks gave Martin a boyish look that made him appear much younger than his fifty-something age bracket. He opened his arms for the hug Clarissa happily gave.

"So sorry to hear about Jaz, my love." Martin kissed her forehead. He glanced toward Waymon. "Has this guy explained that we're all here to help in whatever way we can?"

Clarissa looked over at Waymon, too, and then she nodded.

Martin appeared satisfied, smoothing his hands along Clarissa's sleeves. "Let's get started then."

Elias had another hour or so before his meeting with Clarissa David. His *second* meeting, he recalled and felt the smile coming to his face. He then muttered a curse over his inability to stifle the gesture and wondered what it was about her. Just *her*—not her aunt or any of that drama. Would seeing her under the guise of business be enough to give him the answers he wanted?

Was it fair for him to use business as the excuse?

Elias cursed again and effectively set the thought from his mind. He had arrived at the downtown headquarters of Echols's Bank and Securities. Eli shut down the Navigator's engine and waited—debating.

He reassessed Barker's suspicions and wondered if he could get Cleve Echols to put them to rest.

"One way to find out." He groaned and exited the dark SUV.

* * *

Cleve Echols was as beloved by his staff as he was by his customers, and it showed in the easy manner, laughter and conversation that livened the lobby of the elegantly furnished high-rise. The banking officers who weren't with customers all recognized Elias. They threw up waves and nods but it was mortgage officer Linda Reynolds who actually tugged Eli into her office after she quickly ended a call and rushed out to grab his arm.

"Why didn't you tell me you were coming by?" Linda scolded.

"Spur of the moment. I didn't stop by to take you away from anything."

Linda flushed slightly beneath her light honey-colored complexion. "Now, Eli, you know you're free to take me away from anything—anytime you want to." She looked over her shoulder at the three female co-workers who watched Elias with blatant lust and Linda with sheer venom.

Unperturbed, Linda sent them saucy winks and strolled off with the man they drooled over.

"Get you a drink?" she offered when they were closed inside the office.

"I'm good." Eli sat on the edge of Linda's glass desk. "I want to know how Mr. Cleve's doing."

"That's right—the deal." Linda rested a hand across the open neckline of her shirt. "I'm so sorry that all fell through. He's been very tense lately. I don't think anyone else has really noticed it yet with all the shake-ups we've been having on the real estate end. They've been…unsettling."

"Unsettling?" Eli probed.

Linda bit her lip and sat down in a chair before her desk.

"He didn't sound like himself when we talked on the phone."

Linda blinked a few times and then buried her head as though she were contemplating. Finally, she locked gazes with Elias. "It's not good. Some of our biggest mortgage loans have fallen through and others are on the teetering edge."

"Times are hard." Eli shrugged, playing devil's advocate.

Linda shook her head forebodingly. "That's not what this is."

"Well, everyone knows some of Mr. Cleve's clients don't make their money in the most ordinary ways."

"Humph, ordinary…right…" Linda twisted the thumb ring she wore. "Those *ordinary* clients are being affected too—all of our highest-tiered customers, the ones who truly keep the bank afloat are being affected."

Eli's brow furrowed. "Is it nationwide?"

"Not yet." Linda swallowed. "If I didn't know better, I'd swear our Philly office is being targeted exclusively."

"What's Mr. Cleve sayin' about this?" Eli watched Linda leave the chair, massaging her neck as she paced the length of the windows lining the back wall.

"He hasn't said much of anything. Humph, maybe *I'm* overreacting. Like I said, it's only the Philly offices being affected. Maybe Cleveland knows this is just a hiccup and nothing to worry about."

"Is he around?" Eli asked.

"Taking a long lunch." Linda put a refreshing smile in place. "You're welcome to wait."

Eli glanced at his watch. "Got an appointment." He went to hug Linda. "Tell him I came by, all right?"

When Elias returned to his office, Desmond was there watching with a broad grin.

"Very nice."

Eli tilted his head, smiling curiously. "Are you gonna make me guess?"

"Your two o'clock."

"She's here?" Elias didn't really require a response as he looked toward his closed office door.

"I didn't think you'd mind if I let her wait inside."

"Take the rest of the day, Des," Elias spoke over his shoulder.

"You're sure? You don't need me to take notes or anything?"

Elias stopped when his hand was on the door handle. He gave Desmond the benefit of his bright gaze and sly grin before heading on into the office.

He was able to walk in unnoticed and found Clarissa—to his delight—bending over his desk as she inspected the photographs he kept of his mother along a shelf.

Elias closed the door without making a sound and leaned back next to it. There, he worked his thumb into his palm while studying her dress and sensually shaped legs.

His vivid blue-green stare sketched repeated outlines of her bottom. He drove his thumb a little deeper into his palm, attempting to diminish the ache stemming from a desire to cradle the enticing roundness in his hands—again.

He cleared his throat over a groan and watched her straighten quickly and whirl around to him. The moment she started to explain herself, he moved toward her.

Clarissa blinked and quieted when Elias didn't seem to be of a mind to stop. Not until she was in his arms for the second time that day. He lifted her just a fraction to place her atop his desk and then he cupped her face to deepen their kiss.

Her whimpering and the desperate lunges of her tongue against his drove Elias out of his mind in a matter of seconds.

Clarissa had no time to conjure refusals or second thoughts. She had thought of little else outside of him doing this again. Someplace deep, guilt stirred. Pleasure fevered her brain as opposed to the misery she should have felt on the eve of burying the woman who'd practically raised her.

Yes, continued pleasure fevered her brain and her body while Elias executed his seductive assault. His hands roamed her at will, weighing and squeezing her breasts until they bulged from the lacy bra cups covering them.

The fondling moved to her hips and, upon squeezing her there, Eli lifted Clarissa into his broad solid frame. She, in turn, squeezed his hips between her thighs.

"Clarissa…"

"Hmm…?" Her response was muffled when he kissed her again.

"We're supposed to be working," he spoke amid caressing her tongue with his.

"So? Why did we leave your desk, then?" She smiled when he laughed.

Chapter 7

"Didn't think you'd keep our meeting after this morning," Elias said when he and Clarissa were sharing a sofa. A stack of files sat between them.

"You already think the worst of me," she sang the words while flipping through a folder. "No sense in being a no-show to our meeting and digging myself into a deeper hole."

Elias smiled but didn't look away from the folder he studied, either. "I shouldn't have done that this morning."

"Mmm...but you won't apologize for it?" she guessed.

"Did you enjoy it?"

Thrown by the question, Clarissa's folder slipped from her hands. Lips parted in surprise, she looked over at him.

Elias didn't return her stare. "Did you?" he asked.

She bit her lip momentarily and then nodded once. "Yes."

Eli smiled. "Then, no, I won't apologize for it."

Clarissa leaned over to grab the folder from where it'd fallen. With all the paperwork clipped inside, there were no loose papers to collect. She laid the folder open across her lap again and laughed. "Everything my aunt had goin' on looks like Greek to me."

"You shouldn't be looking at it anyway, not with everything you have on your plate. When's the funeral?"

"Tomorrow." Clarissa pressed her lips together.

"Go home." He rested his arms along the back of the sofa. "This'll keep and look a lot better to you later."

Clarissa's laughter held more humor that time. She closed the folder and stood. Elias followed her every move. He took his time to indulge in a slow, sea-blue scan of her body. He relished the way she smoothed her hands across her hips, bottom and thighs. All the while, he wondered if she did it out of habit, praying to God that she did.

"She left me everything."

Elias's focus was riveted on her words then. Sensing her tension, he tried to gauge her expression.

"Are congrats in order?" he teased, hoping to coax a smile.

Clarissa obliged, but the gesture was only faintly noticeable. "I don't have a clue about *half* of what my aunt's business involved. I was in charge of recruiting dancers for her clubs. I scouted other clubs, some of the girls I approached. Most approached me...."

Elias set aside the paperwork he'd been reviewing,

becoming quickly enthralled by the extent of Clarissa's duties.

"That's a pretty impressive list of responsibilities for strippers—sorry if that sounds harsh," he winced.

"It's true—my duties were very extensive and probably a bit over-the-top given the nature of the business. But my aunt wasn't the heartless home-wrecker everybody thought. The girls who worked the clubs were more than dancers to her. Aunt Jaz believed they could all be more, and it was my job to see that they had those opportunities."

"Sounds like your aunt trusted you with the most important resource of her business."

"Unfortunately it was the *only* part."

"Clarissa?" Eli braced his elbows to his knees and let concern radiate from his voice and expression. "You want to talk about it?"

"I wouldn't know where to start." She massaged her neck with both hands. "I know something was bothering her but I—I was too late to find out what it was."

"It's never too late, babe."

"How can you say that?" Temper flared in Clarissa's brown eyes. "She's gone. The day I met you, I was on my way to discuss all this with her and then she—" She gasped, turning her back on Elias then. She braced her hands atop his desk and bowed her head in a show of defeat.

Eli went to her. Speaking soft words of reassurance, he smoothed his fingers over her bare nape.

"I hope you haven't been blaming yourself for what happened to your aunt."

"I know it's stupid." She closed her eyes as his massage worked its magic. "But I'm finding it hard not to do just that. Eli, she—she sounded so strange on the phone that day."

"Has anyone at the club said anything that would shed light?"

Weariness commanded the slow shake of Clarissa's head.

"Hey." Elias pulled her into a hug.

The gesture stirred emotions for Clarissa which were a far cry from consoling. She inhaled deeply of the cologne clinging to his skin and clothing.

Eli allowed his hands free rein over the body they'd come to crave. Moments later, he was kissing her as if famished for the taste of her.

Moments before her thoughts blurred into the pleasure-scape roused by his touch, she experienced a moment of clarity. She understood what it was that drew her to him. Granted, it was only one of the things but it was by far among the most potent.

Elias Joss had the power to make her forget it all. Her angst regarding the business, guilt over the last moments of Jazmina's life, regrets over the way she'd handled her own life... In his arms, all that registered was the desire to please and be pleasured.

Elias's state of mind wasn't quite as eased. It was true that he forgot everything when Clarissa was near. Once he put his hands on her...all else became unimportant. It was of course a blissful existence. If only he could shake the way he felt his actions were running parallel to his father's. Had Evan Joss experienced the same weakness? Did that explain why he was once ready to cast aside his family for another woman?

And why the hell was he thinking of that at all? Eli rarely wasted time on the memory of his father. Yet when weakness—a thing he had an absolute intolerance for—was the topic, he couldn't help but bring the man to mind. It was those times in which he recalled and dreaded any similarities sharing Evan Joss's blood may have planted.

A chiming sound lilted and Clarissa stiffened. She was slammed to reality as reason and her cellphone tugged her back.

The kiss ended, but Elias didn't release her. Instead, he took the time to fix the smudge of lipstick at her well-kissed mouth. He brushed his mouth across her cheek and stepped away to let her handle the call.

Clarissa took her time about moving. She felt annoyance stir when the ringing chimes resurfaced once the answering service had taken care of the previous call. Whatever it was had to be important, but Clarissa still frowned at the sight of Rayelle's name on the faceplate.

The second call met the same fate as the first, going right to voice mail. Then, there was knocking at the office door.

"Yeah?" Eli called watching Linus stick his head inside the room.

Clarissa felt the phone vibrate again. That time it was a cryptic text from Ray:

Found something—call me!

"Sorry, man, Des wasn't at his desk—" Linus gave a start at finding Clarissa there. "Well, hey!" Linus forgot his partner for the moment and went to welcome Eli's guest.

"The architects are finally satisfied with all the details. They'll be getting started in a month," Linus announced after hugging Clarissa. "They're gonna want to go over it all one more time in case there are any questions. Maybe we can do a dinner or something?" He turned to Elias. "That is, if it's okay with your go-to guy here?"

Eli shrugged, more than a little peeved over Linus's intrusion.

Clarissa smiled. "I can wait for Eli to give me the details, but it sounds fine with me. I, um—" she gave her cell a shake "—I really need to go, Eli. I'm sorry, um, I'll call?"

He nodded. "Sounds good." His rich voice was as steady as his gaze. When the door closed behind Clarissa, his soft expression hardened.

"Eli, man—"

"Save it."

The warning didn't stop Linus from uttering a full-bodied chuckle.

"What is it?" Clarissa frowned over the open book lying flat on the coffee table in Rayelle's office at Jazzy B's.

Ray frowned down at the book, as well. "At first glance, it looks like a list of clients who booked VIP rooms for private dances."

"And on second glance?"

"On second glance, it doesn't look so good, since

money's changed hands." Ray drew her finger along a
row of numbers headed by a dollar sign.

Clarissa massaged the bridge of her nose. "Ray,
please don't tell me this looks like prostitution money."

"I don't know what it is, Clay. 'Specially since I don't
know who this third party is." She tapped the column on
the other side of the dancers' stage names. "For every
one of these clients' names, there's an amount and then
a dancer and then an alphanumeric code. I'm guessing
that's who the real money's going to."

"But money for what? Maybe that's what the alphanumeric entries indicate, you think?"

Ray shrugged. "Given these clients, I'm willin' to
bet there's a good chance it's a shady element at work
here." Ray straightened when she saw Clarissa's frown.
"Clients listed next to the dancers' names are alleged
drug dealers, Clay."

"Crap…" Clarissa massaged a sudden throb near her
temple. "Do you think these girls are involved?"

Ray tugged a lock of hair behind her ear. "Take a
look at those amounts. Would *you* still dance if you
had gotten a payday like that? Maybe the book is set
up this way to make it *look* like some kind of prostitution deal—throw off whoever finds it."

"And how did *you* find it?"

"It was in all those papers of Miss Jaz's. From the
crates I still need to bring out to the house."

Clarissa chewed her thumbnail. "Maybe we should
talk to Waymon."

"I think we should wait 'til we know if this is really
part of something foul."

Massaging her temples again, Clarissa tried to ward off the voice that told her it surely was.

"This is the last thing I need today."

Ray groaned and flopped back on the sofa. "Sorry, Clay."

"No, it's not anything you did. This is all on me."

"Care to dish?" Ray tucked her feet beneath her on the sofa.

Mussing her short hair in frustration, Clarissa displayed a quick frown. "Forget I said anything. I've been weird since my meeting with Elias."

Rayelle smiled and Clarissa rolled her eyes. She made quick work of telling her friend what happened between her and the construction entrepreneur and what *didn't* happen: business.

"That's what we were there for." Clarissa followed Ray's example and tucked her feet beneath her where she claimed the opposite side of the sofa.

"And why are you raking yourself over hot coals about this?"

"Ray, please, I look just like the woman his father almost left his mother for."

"I'm sure you've noticed that Elias Joss is a big enough boy not to have daddy issues."

Clarissa drew up her knees and propped her chin against them. "Whatever happened then really traumatized him, Ray."

"You're afraid it'll affect your relationship."

"Relationship?" Clarissa laughed. "We're far from having one of those, girl."

"Mmm…" Ray studied the stitching along the sofa's arm. "Do you want that?"

"Ray...I barely know him."

"And he's kissed you how many times?"

Clarissa averted her gaze. "Twice."

"And for how long?"

"Stop. I get your point."

"So? Would you like a relationship with him?"

"I don't even know what that is." Clarissa's forlorn response was followed by a weighty sigh.

Rayelle smiled empathetically. "So I guess the real question is, are you ready to find out?"

The overcast day was a fitting accompaniment for the event about to take place. Despite the promise of rain, Clarissa decided on a graveside service for Jazmina. It was a good thing she did, for it seemed that half of Philadelphia turned out for the going home of a woman who was supposedly a pariah.

Clarissa remained stoic on the outside even though her soul was in turmoil.

Too soon...too soon... She kept chanting the phrase in her head while the minister eulogized her aunt. It was unfair, she thought. She felt cheated out of the time she was supposed to have. She and Jaz spent so much time working, still there was much left unsaid.

The words caused Clarissa to stiffen. Yes, there was much left unsaid and there was nothing left to do about it. Jaz was gone and the woman had told her all that needed to be said. Clarissa's aunt wanted her to live and to fall in love.

The service ended with prayer and then attendees proceeded toward the grave to drop single white roses to the top of the casket once it had been lowered into the ground. Each walked by to shake Clarissa's hand. She maintained her politeness but was otherwise un-emotional.

Surprise bloomed in her large, coffee-brown eyes though when Elias took her hand. Clarissa's lips parted to question his presence, but he turned away before she could speak. It was then that she noticed the tall, lovely woman at his side.

"Clarissa David, this is my mother, Lilia Joss," Eli announced.

Clarissa knew her mouth was most likely hanging open in amazement. She also guessed that the reaction was mirrored in her eyes. Nevertheless, she managed to take Lilia's outstretched hand and squeeze it.

"It's very nice to meet you, Mrs. Joss. Thank you so much for coming." Clarissa felt a measure of relief then for Lilia's expression held no traces of disapproval or resentment.

"It's a pleasure, Ms. David." Lilia placed her other gloved hand on Clarissa's arm. "I am sorry for your loss."

Elias took Clarissa's hand again once his mother had moved on. He leaned close and Clarissa wanted to melt when his mouth pressed her ear.

"I'll come see you later?"

She could only nod, unable to resist nudging his mouth.

She had not yet recovered from the shock of meeting Lilia Joss, not to mention the pleasure of Elias's touch, when the final attendee approached to shake her hand. Clarissa turned with a functional smile in place and was struck by the sight of the childlike face before her eyes.

"Rena Johnson," the young woman said. "I used to dance for your aunt's club."

Clarissa let her confusion show. Since she did all the hiring of the dancers, the waif standing before her was all for scrutiny. Clarissa had never met her before. She knew Jaz would have never put such a girl on staff at any of the clubs. Jaz often teased that, if left up to her, she'd have no dancers since she'd try to talk every girl out of getting into that life. The young woman in Clarissa's line of sight would have been a prime candidate for such a chat.

"I'm from Philly," Rena was saying, while wrapping herself tighter in the gray trench she sported. "One night, when the cold and rain finally beat down my guard, Miss J was the only one who let me in when I clawed at her door howling like an idiot!"

Clarissa felt like laughing for the first time that day. "She wasn't afraid of much."

"That's the truth." Rena nodded at whatever memory was making her smile then. "She was a great lady. I'm sorry she's gone."

"Do you still live here in the city?" Clarissa asked.

"Oh, no. Miss J got me out last year." Rena blinked, the look on her thin oval face revealing that she realized how her words must have sounded.

"Things got pretty hairy before I left."

Clarissa studied the girl's face with avid interest. "I don't think we've ever met."

Rena shook her head suddenly. "And I only had a few clients. Miss J didn't want any trouble. I, um—" she shrugged in spite of herself "—I don't exactly look my age. People had questions…"

Clarissa's brow furrowed. "Well, if you were legal age, the subject was pointless. No one could've gotten in trouble and my aunt didn't back down from much, 'specially if she was in the right."

"Well, Mr. Cole had a say in it, so…"

"Was he complaining?"

"Friends of his were."

"Is that why she got you out?"

"Not exactly."

Clarissa's frown cleared, but her suspicions were definitely stoked.

"It's very complicated," Rena gushed, appearing regretful that she'd shared so much.

"Complicated how?" Clarissa pressed. "Did it have to do with Mr. Cole?"

"Not exactly, but since he was Miss J's business manager…it was sort of the last straw when he and his friends told her that I was a problem she didn't need, since there was a client who was getting a little bit, too, um…interested."

Clarissa steeled herself against swaying on the heels of her black pumps. Jazzy B's had never had issues with clients misbehaving. For all *she* knew… Clarissa swallowed around the emotion wadded in her throat. Was this yet another secret Jazmina had kept from her?

"Oh, he wasn't trying to hurt me or nothin'." The girl championed her wayward ex-client. "He was just…kind of eager, you know?"

"I got it." Clarissa twisted her lips while sizing up the issue. "So Jaz was trying to protect you?"

"More for the client's protection. Him being who he is and all."

"Being who he is?"

"He's got a big name, rich, a lot of people know him so…" Rena shrugged and shifted her weight while studying the remaining funeral attendees with increasing apprehension. "I got the feelin' him and Mr. Cole didn't like each other too much. Probably why he gave *me* a hard time. Then there was that other stuff with the money and all."

"Money?" Clarissa's thoughts registered the cryptic notebook Rayelle found.

"Cle hit the roof when he found out about that."

"Cle?"

Rena blinked. "My client, Cleve Echols."

Chapter 8

Clarissa feared she'd wear a groove in the den floor if she paced it much longer. The revealing conversation with the young ex-stripper had ended before she could extract any more choice info. Waymon had called out to her from across the cemetery grounds. Clarissa turned to wave quickly in his direction and when she looked back to Rena, the girl was gone.

She thought of calling Rayelle and brainstorming over what clues the discussion held. That idea held little appeal just then. Clarissa preferred to mull over the strange conversation alone. After only a short while however, her interest in even that had grown thin.

She felt restless and was considering helping herself to Jazmina's impressive stash of liquors when the bell rang.

"Saved…" She cast a lingering look toward the walled bar.

Resolutely, Clarissa turned for the foyer. She fixed the belt on the smart black dress she'd worn for the funeral. She hadn't removed it since returning to the house some three hours earlier.

The conversation with Rena Johnson and her aunt's well-stocked bar begging to be used were causing her to overheat and she broke into a sprint for the front door. Elias stood on the other side.

"Bad time?" Casually, he reached out to smooth a thumb across the corner of her eye. Concern darkened the evocative blue of his stare as he studied her.

Clarissa leaned into the touch. "When isn't it?" she murmured.

"Sounds like you need help." Elias grunted a laugh. "Anything to drink in here?"

Clarissa's laughter was weak but it was there. "Funny you should ask…" she said.

Three brandies later, Elias and Clarissa were sharing the long cream-colored sofa in the living room. Silence had rested easy between them as they enjoyed the fine, dark liquor from crystal snifters. The golden light from the lamps at each corner of the room emphasized the cozy charm of the space.

Clarissa's eyelids felt heavy soon after the first drink and she gave in to letting them settle down more than once. She apologized when it happened after the fifth time but decided Elias was equally to blame.

After their second brandy, he had pulled her legs across his lap and started to rub her calves. Clarissa eased out of her drowsy state each time his hands ventured up over her thighs.

"What are we doing, Eli?" she queried in a slow voice.

He smirked. "Right this minute?" When she only responded with a stare, he shrugged and let his head rest back on the sofa.

Clarissa bit her lip while drawing courage to ask her next question. "Why did your mother come to the funeral?"

He shrugged again, and gave a tug to the open collar of his gray shirt. "It's how she is."

She shook her head in wonder. "Paying her respects to a woman who disrespected her in the most heinous way?"

"My father disrespected her, too, and yet she slept with him every night he came to her bed." The corner of his sensually sculpted mouth tilted into a grim smile.

"It all still bothers you," she noted.

"Not much." Eli was far from buzzed, but the liquor had relaxed him enough to make it difficult to mask true emotion from his face.

"I think she'll love him forever," he confessed of his mother. "They grew up together. I think she still believes the sun rises and sets with the man, despite the hell he took her through."

"They were married." Clarissa followed Eli's lead and let her head rest on the sofa, as well. "They bonded over things you'll never know about—things your mom's probably forgotten about even. I guess it takes a lot to stop loving someone."

"You've got lots of experience with that, I guess?" Eli asked without looking her way.

"I'm happy to say that I've got none."

"But some?"

Clarissa lifted her head. "None." She judged his reaction.

Eli looked over at her then. His extraordinary eyes were narrowed and accusing. "No need to lie." The accusation in his stunning blues turned incredulous. "How is that possible?"

She put her head down again. "Aunt J kept me very busy."

"You didn't spend your entire life working for the woman!" He laughed, and then tilted his head inquisitively. "What about college? High school?"

"Jaz stressed *focusing on my grades.*"

"What'd your parents stress?"

Clarissa's mouth curved downward as her lovely face adopted a shadow. "My mother died giving birth to me. My father raised me but I spent every summer with Jaz. *Every* summer of my life."

"Jesus…Clarissa, you've never lived."

She dismissed his revelation with a wave. "I can promise you that I've lived a lot."

"So you've had your share of men but none serious enough to be long lasting or to fall in love with?" he surmised, yet tensed inwardly at the mere possibility of another man touching her. He didn't know what to make of such a reaction to a time before either knew the other existed. Instead, he set his thoughts on Jazmina Beaumont and discovered he had another reason to despise the woman. She'd made a workhorse of her own niece, forcing Clarissa to walk the straight and narrow while she delighted in her own wild existence....

Clarissa continued to consider Elias's demeanor. The set to his striking profile had her very curious. When his bright gaze shifted her way, she repeated her question.

"What are we doing, Eli?" She pressed her lips together, silently willing his answer.

"I can't tell you what we're doing, Clari," he said finally, shortening her name while watching his fingertips tap out a rhythm across the top of her foot. "All that I can tell you is, when I'm with you, I don't have another damn thing on my mind. When you're not with me, the only thing on my mind is you. I don't know what that means, but I know I like it." He released his hold on her calf for one across her wrist. Without giving her the chance to think, he lifted her over to straddle his lap. The scene turned explosive in the time frame of a few seconds.

"Stop me," he said when they were in the depths of a full-blown, wet and lusty kiss.

"Are you serious?" she gasped and cried out when he laid her down on the sofa.

"You don't know me, Clarissa." His deep voice seemed to resonate on an impossibly lower level. "I can be moody and possessive," he cautioned as his mouth explored the length of her still-clothed body. "Ruthless if that's what it takes to get my way."

"No need to be ruthless." She sighed, subtly arching each time his mouth hit a new spot. "You can have your way." Her mind was numb with wanting him.

Elias kissed her to shut her up then. Silently, he told himself that she had no idea what she was saying to him. He'd thought of little else besides having "his way" with her since he'd seen her. Hell, he'd come there that night with those very thoughts at the front of his mind, hadn't he? The things he wanted to do with her would be most taxing on her lovely body if she gave him free rein. Most taxing and most enjoyable.

"Stop me, Clarissa...."

"No...." She was wriggling out of the blouse-styled bodice of the dress.

The movement of her plump almond-brown breasts, clad in the lacy black of her bra, dissolved Eli's restraint. Clarissa may have been disturbed by the power of his touch if she didn't want him so badly.

Her heart pounded something fierce in her ears as he stripped her of everything else she wore. On the wide sofa, he subjected her to an intense session of foreplay.

Clarissa felt she was outside herself when the sound of her voice touched her ears. She was apologizing to Eli when his actions brought her to a sudden climax.

"Don't worry about it," he spoke in the process of tongue-kissing her neck. "You're about to make it up to me," he promised her.

He raised above her, removing his shirt to reveal an awesomely chiseled chest. Unzipping his pants, he removed condoms from his pocket and freed himself from silver-gray boxers. Testosterone zipped through his veins along with pulsing blood. He couldn't think straight and needed to be inside her quickly and deeply.

He criticized himself for rushing. He vowed to make it up to her. He'd spend all night making it up to her. He claimed her in one swift plunging thrust and went ice cold when her shriek pierced his ears.

Eli hissed a curse that bordered on pleasure and dev-
astation. The truth of what had just happened registered
in his mind but it was shrouded in an erotic mist that he
was content with. He tried to speak her name but could
scarcely manage sound.

"Don't—don't stop," she said in a manner that was
just as strained.

Elias chose to listen to her and ignore the anguish
laced in her expression. It wasn't a difficult choice to
make considering that he was already painfully aroused
for her. He moved slightly and lost the ability to keep
his head lifted. Sensation was shuddering through him
as his sex invaded more of her tightness.

He could tell that she was tense from the pain and he
set out to quickly dispel that. Eli feared she'd draw blood
from her lip, she was clenching it just that tightly. Her
hands were clenched, as well, balled against the broad
wall of his muscle packed chest.

Clarissa hadn't anticipated the pain. She'd lost herself
in the fantasy of the ways that a man, with a body like
Elias Joss's, could usher her into a delight she'd denied
herself for far too long.

The pain was still at its peak, though below the surface of that pain, she could feel another kind of throb.
One that was heavy, intense and exquisite. Elias had
lowered his head to her chest. His nose outlined the
curve of one breast, before his tongue charted a simi-
lar path about her nipple.

Discomfort, though a bit less intense, stemmed from
the junction of her thighs when he pressed his wide
hands against them and slightly lifted himself above
her. Keeping her in place on the sofa, Elias moved with

a deft expertise which beckoned the erotic throb to rise from below the surface of her pain. The pleasure surged like a potent blast. At first, Clarissa could only snuggle deeper into the sofa cushions as her lips parted for a moan that had yet to sound.

Gradually, her hands uncurled from clenched fists. She began to rake her nails ever-so-lightly across taut muscles that flexed beneath the flawless caramel tone of his skin.

Clarissa bit her lip again just as the moan brought sound into the quiet room. Elias was reluctant to abandon the nipple he'd suckled into a hard, glistening peak but he wanted to watch her taking what he gave her.

His hypnotic ocean-blue stare was slitted as he took delight in her beauty. The pout of her full lips had him especially captivated. He couldn't help but wonder how they'd feel in comparison to the part of her anatomy he was blessed to be exploring.

The mere thought of it all caused his erection to stiffen anew, but Elias willed himself against erupting. The least he could do was to ensure that her pleasure equaled or surpassed his own. Arrogance curved his mouth into a smirk. It would take quite a lot for her pleasure to surpass his own. He didn't believe anything else could rival the feel of being inside her.

Soft whimpering crept from Clarissa's mouth as her pleasure intensified. She couldn't even recall that pain had ever been a part of it. Instinctively, her hips rotated and lifted beneath Eli's. The move stirred the most delicious reaction. Her body was in tune to the rhythm he stoked with the length and thickness of his shaft. The organ filled and stretched her to capacity. Her breathing started to resemble pants and every part of her trembled.

Eli's mouth grazed the line of her collarbone and Clarissa marveled in response to her sensitivity to his touch. Again, she bit her lip, whimpering when the satiny petals guarding her sex tensed sweetly around him.

Eli tightened his grip on her thigh while adding speed to his thrusts. "Clarissa..." he groaned into her neck and gave himself over to the effect she had on him. His big frame tensed and then shuddered as he came hard. Gripping her tightly, he muttered a lurid, complimentary curse in reference to her curves filling his palms.

Their combined breathing filled the room. Clarissa wanted to turn her face into Eli's neck and absorb the fantastic smell of his cologne but she dared not move. She relished his arms about her and she didn't want that feeling to end.

Such was not to be. Eli withdrew only after inhaling the intoxicating scent from the crook of Clarissa's neck. She winced as his weight left her and again when she inched up on the sofa and drew her legs beneath her.

Elias left the sofa, his back to Clarissa as he ran a hand across his face and massaged his neck. Then he reached over, collected the discarded dress and tossed it on her nude form. He next disposed of the condom, fixed his pants and jerked into his shirt.

Instead of reclaiming his place on the sofa, he sat on the coffee table to face her directly.

"How are you a virgin?" he inquired simply, albeit firmly.

Clarissa parted her lips and then sighed and attempted to lighten the mood when she shrugged. "Well…I'm not."

Elias was clearly unamused by the tease. Clarissa cleared her throat in acknowledgment of his narrowed, vivid gaze and the fierce sharpening of his handsome face. His eyes were focused and unwavering as he watched her. It was unnecessary to say that he was livid.

"Why did you let me do that to you?"

"Do what?" His hushed tone had been as unnerving as his stare but Clarissa wouldn't allow herself to be cowed. "Elias?" she challenged, lifting her chin boldly when his mouth crooked into a smirk.

"You think this is funny?" he asked.

Clarissa scooted to the edge of the sofa. She kept the dress pressed to her chest in an attempt to preserve a hint of modesty.

"I don't think it's funny at all, but it's damn well confusing. Why are you so upset? Because I didn't tell you?"

Elias's smirk segued into a smile. The gesture however lent an even more dangerous air to his expression. "We'll get to that, Ms. David." He slid a disgusted look toward the sofa.

"How could you let me…have you like that on a couch?"

Clarissa leaned back against the sofa arm and considered the question while studying the area where her deflowering had occurred. The memory of it stirred a tingle in her newly awakened sex and her lips parted in preparation for a gasp.

"Clarissa."

Eli's voice disintegrated the rosy memories stirring her arousal. She rolled her eyes toward him.

"Is there a rule about where it happens?" She flinched when he bolted from the coffee table and cupped her chin.

"Not on a damn sofa."

Clarissa thought a growl would have sounded more inviting than the way he voiced the statement. Regardless of that, Clarissa was melting as he stood there glaring down at her, undoubtedly pissed off. The mixture of sweat and cologne on him was an intoxicating brew that brought just a hint of a flutter to her thick lashes. Her fingertips ached to graze the exposed skin visible beneath his open shirt.

She was hungry for another kiss. Boldly, she allowed him to spy her need when her eyes traveled up from his chest to settle on his mouth. They lingered there while she bit her lip and then soothed the area with her tongue.

Elias wasn't immune. His body hadn't stopped reacting to her at all. The silent admission only heated his simmering temper. He rolled his eyes, cursed softly, but fiercely and moved away from Clarissa as if she were a flame he'd gotten too close to.

"Eli—"

"It *is* supposed to be special," he argued.

"It was," she vowed.

Elias either didn't believe her or he just wasn't in the mood to hear anything more from her. He waved off her words and felt the pockets of his black carpenter-style trousers. He jingled the keys he found there and buttoned his shirt while heading for the armchair where a pair of suede hiking boots had been tossed. Collecting them, he strolled barefoot from the living room. "Not the way I do things, Clarissa," he called over his shoulder on the way out.

Chapter 9

Rook Lourdess rubbed the ache from his jaw even as he grinned toward Elias, who was doubled over across the ring.

"Who is she?" Rook asked, his gravelly voice sounding very much out of breath as he observed his old friend.

Eli frowned. "Say what?"

"Don't try it." Rook waved a gloved hand dismissively. "You almost killed me. The only men who hit like that are ones on the outs with their bedmate or the ones who can't figure out how to get her into bed yet."

"Well…" Eli leaned against the ropes and massaged the back of his neck. "Neither of those pertain to me."

"But a member of the opposite sex *is* involved? Who is she?" Rook asked again, taking Elias grimace as a confirming answer.

"Clarissa David."

"You don't have to lie about it."

"I didn't lie."

Rook's thick brows joined when he frowned in concentration as if he were trying to envision something. "No way." He settled the matter with a quick shake of his head and another dismissive wave of a gloved hand.

"Have you met her?" Elias asked.

"Once or twice. When the guys were getting the layout of the place for a private party at her aunt's club." Rook's nationally known firm staffed security for some of the most high-profile events in the country. The rigorous training Rook put his men through yielded such coveted results that he'd captured the attention of Hollywood directors and pro athletes alike.

"You're serious," Rook breathed. "She looks just like her aunt."

Eli smiled. "Yeah, I noticed."

"So what's that about?"

Eli rubbed his fingers through the short waves covering his head. "It's about me not knowing what the hell I'm doing."

"Understandable." Rook wrapped his arms around the ropes and leaned back on the ring. "The woman's a dime if I ever saw one."

"Tell me about it." Elias began to pace the ring in the private underground gym of Lourdess Securities. "She's like a drug."

"Again—understood." Rook's grin sparked a dimple. "That face and all those curves…when I first saw her I thought she was a dancer in that damn club." Rook sighed, taking in his friend's distressed expression. "So are you gonna tell me what's goin' on?"

"Right away—once I understand it."

"Problems?"

"Complications," Eli stated, his mind still reeling a little over the events of the previous evening. "I don't want to hurt her, Rook."

"Yeah…" Rook paced the ring once back and forth. "Most of us don't set out to hurt the women we pursue, but we do it anyway." He rubbed his neck as if some unforeseen tension had suddenly landed there.

"There's that, too."

Elias's closed remark told Rook that he wouldn't get much more clarification in the matter. Therefore, he decided to stick with what seemed to be doing the most good. "You up for more sparring?"

"Think your jaw can take it?" Eli's extraordinary eyes sparkled with humor and challenge.

"Only one way to find out." Rook shrugged.

Seconds later the two men reengaged.

Clarissa raised her hands to ward off the insistent shoves against her shoulders. Someplace deep in her subconscious she thought she heard Rayelle's voice. Blindly, she reached for a pillow to pull over her head and douse the sound.

Rayelle wouldn't give up. She only pushed harder against Clarissa's shoulders. At the first signs of her waking, Ray gave her a quick jerk.

"Don't even think about going back to sleep."

"What?" Clarissa frowned and fought to do as Ray had ordered. "What's wrong…?"

"Why don't *you* tell *me* that? Are you all right?" Ray moved closer to the bed and frowned suspiciously.

"Yeah…" Clarissa slowly braced her weight on an elbow. "Yeah, I'm fine."

Rayelle appeared doubtful and Clarissa took note. "Why?"

"Do you remember that we were supposed to get together this morning and go over more of Miss J's things?"

"Oh." Clarissa covered her mouth with the back of her hand. "Sorry," she said during a hearty yawn.

"Don't worry about it." Ray sat on the edge of the bed. "I know the funeral was rough. Did you do all right, last night?"

"What are you getting at?" The reference to "last night" was an effective agitator.

"Now hold on." Ray lifted her hands in mock defense. "I know it was a rough day—it was for *me,* too. Then I come over here this morning and there's blood on the sofa—"

"God." Mortified, Clarissa brought both hands to her mouth that time.

"Honey, what happened?" Ray pulled down Clarissa's hands and squeezed them.

"It—" Clarissa grimaced and gave Ray's hands a shake. "It's not what you think. I'm fine. Elias…he came over last night."

Rayelle straightened. "Oh." She let go of Clarissa's hands. "Um…well…am I, uh, interrupting?"

Clarissa's laughter held faint traces of sorrow. "He left right after we…finished."

"Clay…" Ray gasped, her fair skin darkening when

she flushed. "That's why the blood…well, I…" She blinked rapidly and began to rub damp palms across jean-clad thighs.

"I won't be crass and ask how it was. I know a book shouldn't be judged by its cover." She gushed suddenly, "But, Clay, damn, that's a wager I'd guess is a safe bet. At least tell me if I'm right?"

Clarissa closed her eyes, settling back to nod against the pillows. Tingles of arousal stirred on the memory. They nudged against faint pulses of pain—another reminder of what else had transpired the night before.

"I'm surprised he left." Ray studied the bedroom as though she expected evidence to the contrary. "Man makes a discovery like *that* about a woman, it's usually hard for him to stay away from her."

"Well, about that." Clarissa inched up in the bed. "He wasn't all too pleased by the discovery."

Rayelle kept quiet, waiting.

Clarissa mopped her face with her hand. "I didn't tell him before we…"

Ray's gasping filled the room. "Clay, why?"

"I wasn't thinking about that—only about what I wanted and how much I wanted it from *him* and how long I've pretended I was all right without it." She rolled her eyes and rested against the headboard. "I was afraid he'd stop if I told him."

"Finally a breakthrough. Honesty at last."

"Ray, please…"

"So what happened after?"

"Hell, Ray, what do you think?"

"Oh, let's see…" Ray rested on her elbow propped on the bed. "Considering the state of the sofa, I'd say

KIMANI
ROMANCE

An Important Message from the Publisher

Dear Reader,

Because you've chosen to read one of our fine novels, I'd like to say "thank you"! And, as a special way to say thank you, I'm offering to send you two more Kimani™ Romance novels and two surprise gifts—absolutely FREE! These books will keep it real with true-to-life African American characters that turn up the heat and sizzle with passion.

Please enjoy the free books and gifts with our compliments...

Glenda Howard
For Kimani Press™

Peel off Seal and Place Inside...

FREE GIFTS
EDITOR'S SEAL
THANK YOU

K-ROM-13

We'd like to send you two free books to introduce you to Kimani™ Romance books. These novels feature strong, sexy women, and African-American heroes that are charming, loving and true. Our authors fill each page with exceptional dialogue, exciting plot twists, and enough sizzling romance to keep you riveted until the very end!

KIMANI ROMANCE...LOVE'S ULTIMATE DESTINATION

Your two books have combined cover price of $12.50 in the U.S. $14.50 in Canada, but are yours **FREE!**

We'll even send you two wonderful surprise gifts. You can't lose!

THE EDITOR'S "THANK YOU" FREE GIFTS INCLUDE:

➤ Two Kimani™ Romance Novels
➤ Two exciting surprise gifts

YES! I have placed my Editor's "thank you" Free Gifts seal in the space provided at right. Please send me 2 FREE Books, and my 2 FREE Mystery Gifts. I understand that I am under no obligation to purchase anything further, as explained on the back of this card.

PLACE
FREE GIFTS
SEAL
HERE

168/368 XDL FV2H

Please Print

FIRST NAME

LAST NAME

ADDRESS

APT.#   CITY

STATE/PROV.   ZIP/POSTAL CODE

Thank You!

Offer limited to one per household and not applicable to series that subscriber is currently receiving.

Your Privacy—The Harlequin® Reader Service is committed to protecting your privacy. Our Privacy Policy is available online at www.ReaderService.com or upon request from the Harlequin Reader Service. We make a portion of our mailing list available to reputable third parties that offer products we believe may interest you. If you prefer that we not exchange your name with third parties, or if you wish to clarify or modify your communication preferences, please visit us at www.ReaderService.com/consumerschoice or write to us at Harlequin Reader Service Preference Service, P.O. Box 9062, Buffalo, NY 14269. Include your complete name and address.

▲ Detach card and mail today. No stamp needed.

©2012 HARLEQUIN ENTERPRISES LIMITED ® and ™ are trademarks owned and used by the trademark owner and/or its licensee. Printed in the U.S.A.

K-ROM-13

HARLEQUIN® READER SERVICE—Here's How It Works:

Accepting your 2 free books and 2 free gifts (gifts valued at approximately $10.00) places you under no obligation to buy anything. You may keep the books and gifts and return the shipping statement marked "cancel." If you do not cancel, about a month later we'll send you 4 additional books and bill you just $4.94 each in the U.S. or $5.49 each in Canada. That is a savings of at least 21% off the cover price. Shipping and handling is just 50¢ per book in the U.S. and 75¢ per book in Canada.* You may cancel at any time, but if you choose to continue, every month we'll send you 4 more books, which you may either purchase at the discount price or return to us and cancel your subscription.
*Terms and prices subject to change without notice. Prices do not include applicable taxes. Sales tax applicable in N.Y. Canadian residents will be charged applicable taxes. Offer not valid in Quebec. All orders subject to credit approval. Credit or debit balances in a customer's account(s) may be offset by any other outstanding balance owed by or to the customer. Offer available while quantities last. Books received may not be as shown. Please allow 4 to 6 weeks for delivery.

If offer card is missing write to: Harlequin Reader Service, P.O. Box 1867, Buffalo, NY 14240-1867 or visit www.ReaderService.com

BUSINESS REPLY MAIL
FIRST-CLASS MAIL   PERMIT NO. 717   BUFFALO, NY

POSTAGE WILL BE PAID BY ADDRESSEE

HARLEQUIN READER SERVICE
PO BOX 1867
BUFFALO NY 14240-9952

NO POSTAGE
NECESSARY
IF MAILED
IN THE
UNITED STATES

that's where the deed was done—or undone. He strikes me as a man who wouldn't be too pleased about that."

"I can't believe he overreacted that way," Clarissa whispered.

"Overreacted?" Ray sat up. "Girl, are you saying that you can't see the significance of his pissed-offness?"

Muttering a curse then, Clarissa whipped back the covers and started straightening her side of the bed. "I know I should have told him. I know that, Ray, all right?"

"Honey, he sees your aunt as the whore who ruined his family and then he goes and practically treats you like one by having sex—*for the first time*—with you on the sofa and taking your virginity besides."

Clarissa lost her ability to grip the covers. She walked around and settled down next to Rayelle on the bed. "Stupid," she said in reference to herself. "I didn't feel that he was treating me that way."

"But you don't have all that history floating around in your mind like he does." Ray studied the lifelines in her palms. "Things happened in my childhood I know *I'll* never get over. I imagine it's the same for him."

Clarissa reached over to entwine her fingers with Ray's. She realized there were things in the woman's past that would forever be alien to her. Still, Rayelle's words made her think more critically of what had happened between her and Elias and the way he may have perceived it.

She began, for a time, to put in an efficient yet pensive attempt at making the bed. "Do you think he'll lose respect for me over the way I handled this—or *didn't* handle this?"

Ray smiled while shaking her head. "You waited until you were thirty-three to lose your virginity—I'd say your respect level's still intact."

Clarissa returned Rayelle's smile in the span of five seconds. In silence they joined forces to finish the bed and then settle down on the surface again.

"Why'd you sleep with him?" Ray asked, and then rolled her eyes. "Back up. Dumb question. Why was *he* the one? Lord knows you weren't a virgin because no one wanted to sleep with you."

Clarissa lay flat on the bed and looked up at the gilded high ceiling. "I could say it's because he's sexy as sin without even trying or because he doesn't feel the need to make a big show over how intelligent he is—he just…is. *Or* I could say it's because he's very incredible to look at."

"Damn straight." Ray sighed, joining Clarissa over several moments of wicked laughter.

Clarissa drew up her knees and bumped her fists against her thighs. "I guess the truth is that there's something genuine about him. All my life I've had the feeling that the people closest to me were keeping things.… Whether it was to hide their guilt or to protect me, I still felt it. I felt it from my father, the family, Jaz.… I don't think I know anyone who can truly say 'what you see is what you get.'"

"Thanks." Ray pursed her lips.

"Sorry." Clarissa nudged her foot to Ray's thigh.

"In light of what you just said, Clay, I hope you don't think that a man like Elias Joss doesn't have secrets. Maybe he just knows how to hide them better than the rest of us."

"That isn't what I mean." Clarissa spread her hands out over the bed. "I think he knows who he is. Good or bad, he doesn't feel the need to apologize for it. He's not ashamed or proud of it but it's part of him and he'll do what it takes to live with it."

She covered her face in a pillow. "Don't ask me how I know that," she said after pulling away the pillow. "It's just a feeling."

Ray nodded. "Well, it was a strong enough feeling to make you give him the most special part of yourself."

"Yeah." Clarissa closed her eyes for a long while. "Now I have to wait and see if that was a mistake or the best decision I ever made."

Elias got to work that morning to discover that Desmond had stepped away from his desk. He checked his watch and decided to hang around. He needed the information he'd asked Desmond to dig up before he could make an unexpected stop later that day.

He headed into his office, figuring he'd just mill about before digging into any additional business. He was heading for the sofa, but switched paths grimacing as memories surfaced. The workout with Rook had helped...while it was in progress. Now, he was back to thinking of Clarissa.

Back to thinking of Clarissa? Thinking of her was all he'd done since he'd met her. Thoughts of her—of having her—had taken up most of his consideration. Now, mere thoughts had transported themselves into reality.

She was a virgin—*was* being the key word and he'd held himself totally to blame. Blame? Yes, he thought, *blame* was the appropriate word there. Sure, she could have told him—given him a heads-up about what he was in for. Would it have mattered? Unless she had asked him to stop, would he have?

It was moot anyway. What was done was done. He couldn't give back what he had taken—what she had given. Elias shook off the qualification. Taken or given wasn't the issue anyway. The only thing that mattered was how insatiable he was for her. His need for her seemed to overrule everything else.

That was the true issue for him, wasn't it? Loss of control.

"Yeah?" Eli called when a quick knock intruded on his thoughts.

"Sorry, boss." Desmond rushed inside.

"Find anything?"

"I'm surprised Mr. Grant didn't have this—you said you met with him the other day, right?" At Eli's nod, Desmond shrugged one shoulder beneath his khaki shirt.

"So you found something."

Desmond ripped a sheet from the 8x11–size legal pad he carried and handed it to his boss. "Names of Mr. Echols's investors for the new bank," he explained.

"All women? Or am I wrong?"

"Nope, you're right—all sixty-one of them."

"Anything else? I recognize some of these names."

"Yeah, me, too." Desmond drew a hand through his dreads and looked toward the list. "Three or four of 'em at least. All of them makin' shakes around town. There're a couple of lawyers and an anchor from Mr. Grant's station. That's why I'm surprised he didn't have the names somewhere. The rest of them…it's anybody's guess."

"Right." Elias gave the page a thump with his middle finger. "Thanks, Des, for taking care of this. Do I want to know exactly *how* you got this?"

Desmond posted up on the balls of his feet and looked humorously smug. "We executive assistants are a close-knit group, sir. Good enough?"

Eli grinned and flashed a wink. "Good enough."

When Desmond was gone, Eli scanned the names again.

That afternoon, Clarissa was shaking hands with Detective Sophia Hail.

"Call me Sophie, please," the tall, dark woman urged once she and Clarissa had taken their seats at a table in the bar and grill where they'd agreed to meet for lunch.

"I was very sorry to hear about Miss Jazmina."

"Thank you." Clarissa made a pretense at straightening the rolled napkin of silverware.

Sophie's lovely features were drawn taut with tension. "My, um…my family didn't have the best relationship with her."

"I see." Inwardly, Clarissa bristled and started straightening the silverware more diligently. "I'm learning that my aunt didn't seem to have the best *history* with much of anyone."

Sophie smiled and tucked soft, spiral curls behind her ear. "This particular history probably isn't about what you're thinking. It's got to do with my sister instead of my father." Like most everyone in Philadelphia,

Sophie knew all too well about Jazmina Beaumont's romantic involvements with attached men.

Curiosity bloomed on the perfect oval of Clarissa's face. Her hands stilled over the table.

"My sister was a cocktail waitress for your aunt back in the day before she was…discovered."

Clarissa's curiosity merged into understanding. "Hail…your sister's not…Viva Hail, is it?"

Sophie's dark gray eyes narrowed to an amused squint. "The one and only…"

Viva Hail had gone from a commercial actress to leading lady in the span of three years. Not bad for a black girl from Philly with no previous acting experience. Viva's rise to the top had been well documented by the media. When tabloids, TV and magazines tried to make a scandal of her past employment at Jazzy B's, Viva took the possibility off the table. She proudly acknowledged her time there. She often thanked Jaz for hiring her and subsequently making her big break possible.

"Your aunt always felt bad for putting a rift between V and the family. I think that may be why she came to me with this. What people thought meant a lot to her."

"Excuse me, *this?*"

Sophie shook her head. "Right, um, it's what I wanted to see you about. Clarissa, did your aunt ever talk to you about…changes she wanted to make with the club?"

"Well, we're going through some remodeling now, so there's that.…"

"I see." Sophie tapped a thumbnail to the dent in her chin, considering Clarissa's response when she blinked at the man approaching the table. She watched Santigo Rodriguez greeting her lunch partner.

When Tigo spotted Sophie, his easygoing, animated demeanor took on an obvious somberness.

"Hey, Tig." Sophie harbored as much somberness in her quiet greeting.

Clarissa observed the first glimpse of something being subdued in the detective's confident no-nonsense manner. Not surprising, Clarissa reasoned. Santigo Rodriguez could send any woman off-kilter.

Tigo got himself in check and reluctantly looked away from Sophie before he smiled down at Clarissa again.

"Sorry for interrupting you. Good to see you, Clarissa. Sophie," he added softly before moving on.

Clarissa decided it'd be best to nudge the conversation along. Even so, she wouldn't have been opposed to finding out more about the drama residing between the statuesque detective and one of Elias's partners.

"Was my aunt in some kind of trouble with the club?"

Sophie's attention refocused. "Not exactly." She rested her elbows on the table. "But she was concerned that something troubling was going on there."

"And she came to you with it?" Clarissa couldn't stop the tightness from creeping into her voice. How much more had Jaz kept from her?

"Clarissa, I think she would have told you if she'd had more to go on." Sophie leaned in a little as if to assure Clarissa of the fact.

"My aunt kept a lot more than this to herself, Detective." Clarissa cradled her face in her hands. "I don't know why I should be surprised by this."

"Well, if it helps to know, I think she may've had a breakthrough of some kind with her suspicions."

Clarissa sat back and recalled the strange notebook of dancer's names, alphanumeric numbers and dollar amounts. "What did she say to you?"

"Nothing specific, but I think she was ready to come through with more than she already had."

"Which was?"

"I met her one day at the club." Sophie traced the stitching along the cuff of her dark blazer. "She told me that she wanted to change it."

"The remodeling?"

Sophie slowly shook her head. "I think it was about more than that. I got the idea that she wanted to change the whole…philosophy of it."

"Wait a minute." Clarissa laughed and folded her arms over her chest. "Are you saying that she wanted to change it from a strip club?"

"That's exactly what I'm trying to tell you."

"When was this?"

"Almost five months ago." Sophie waved off the waiter who tried for a second time to take their drink orders. "The meeting ended with Miss Jaz stressing that she'd always tried to run a clean business, for what it was worth. She said there were those who preferred it dirty and they'd make it hard for her to change it."

"Did you meet again after that?"

"Mmm-hmm, we talked about the club again—it wasn't exactly police business, but I didn't mind." Sophie sipped the water that had been waiting when she and Clarissa took their places at the table. "After the crap hit the fan between Viva and our folks, I pretty much lost contact with my sister. I realized how little I knew about her and talking to Miss Jazz helped.

"She wanted to turn the place into a dancing studio. She talked about all the true talent in the club, said more girls should have the chance to be discovered like V was. She wanted to do more to make that possible for them." Sophie trailed a nail along the sweating glass. "We met a few more times after that—conversation was pretty much the same and then a few weeks ago, Miss J called saying she'd figured out whatever was going on. She said she wanted us to meet and that she wanted *you* there."

Clarissa could do nothing to mask her stupefied expression.

Sophie took pity. "I'm sorry to lay all this on you so soon after…"

"It's fine. I needed to hear it."

"Your aunt was sure that she was on to something. I don't think she'd have called me unless that 'something' was criminal." Sophie reached into an inside pocket on the fitted blazer she wore. "I'd like you to call me if anything weird sticks out to you." She slid her card across the table and squeezed Clarissa's hand when she accepted it.

"Thanks for seeing me." Sophie smiled and left the table.

Clarissa held the card in one hand while she gripped the table in the other and willed her tears not to make an appearance.

Chapter 10

Elias decided to take the mysterious list of names to Barker and get his impressions or suspicions…. Eli figured it couldn't hurt to have a few more facts in place when he spoke to Cleve Echols again.

Talking to Barker, however, was the last thing on his mind when he arrived at the Hemming Bar and Grill. He saw Clarissa strolling past the double doors of the establishment. He watched as she headed for the curb as though she were about to hail a cab. He hit the gas on the Navigator, rolling to a stop alongside her before she could lift a hand.

Too stunned to even speak his name, Clarissa only stood there blinking. Her mouth was parted in surprise.

"Where to?" he inquired simply, staring at her from behind a pair of sunglasses that shielded his ice-blue gaze.

"Home," Clarissa said even though she was planning to meet Rayelle back at the club.

"Get in."

She didn't refuse or hesitate to accept his request.

Elias waited on her to get settled in the passenger seat, allowing him to survey the seductive shape of her legs and the appealing plumpness of her thighs which were bared when the wind caught the flaring hemline of the powder-blue dress she wore.

"Your aunt's place, the hotel or the apartment you keep uptown?"

She was speechless over the fact that he knew of the apartment she mostly used for storage, but she made no comment. He probably knew every square inch of the city and who occupied it, she reasoned.

"The hotel's fine," she said in a small voice. Silently, she asked herself what the hell she thought she was doing. Hoping for a repeat of last night? What would he think of her if he knew that's exactly where her thoughts were centered? She drifted back to the present time to see him bypass the hotel exit. She was sure it hadn't been a mistake and decided to wait to see what he had in mind.

An unfamiliar acoustic piece floated from the speakers and worked its much-needed magic on her frazzled nerves. As if obeying some unspoken hypnotic suggestion, Clarissa leaned back on the headrest and urged her mind to calm.

Elias stopped the Navigator in the reserved spot outside the townhome he kept just inside the city limits.

He silenced the ignition and waited for Clarissa to ask why they were there and where *there* was.

No sound emerged from the passenger side of the vehicle. It was only then that he discovered she had fallen asleep.

With his striking stare narrowed to a blue-green line, Elias angled his large frame on the seat and watched her doze. The provocative set of his wide mouth was curved into a faint smile. He outlined every inch of her lovely almond-toned face—first with his eyes and then with his fingertips which found Clarissa's mouth to be the most inviting stop along the tour.

She shifted slightly on the seat. The tip of her tongue darted out to lick her lips, brushing the pad of his thumb in the process.

Elias groaned a curse. "Clarissa? Clarissa, wake up." He squeezed her thigh, lingering much longer than he knew was necessary. His fingers curled into the flesh of her upper thigh and he studied the changes in her expression as she reacted to his touch.

"Clarissa." His clear baritone was softer and the squeeze to her thigh became a self-serving massage. All the while, he watched her face as though he was in awe of her—and he was.

He suddenly realized what was fueling his fascination—his infatuation with her. It wasn't that she looked like the woman who reminded him of the worst time in his life. She looked like the woman he was falling in love with.

"How the hell did *that* happen?" he muttered.

"Eli." Clarissa's lashes drifted apart just barely, she was still mostly asleep.

"Hey?" Eli sat closer, kissing her ear once, twice… "Clarissa?"

He left the SUV and came around to make a more effective stab at waking her. Briefly, he played with the idea of carrying her inside, but he quickly decided against that. Not that she couldn't use the lift. He dismissed the arrogant boast that taunted of her exhaustion having to do with last night's encounter.

Eli's nudges finally pulled Clarissa from her slumber. When her eyes opened and her gaze fully focused, she gave a start at finding him there.

"Had a stop to make first," he explained before she could ask. "Didn't want to leave you out here asleep."

"You passed the exit." Her words carried on a drowsy brogue.

"Did I?"

Clarissa was still too groggy and drunk on his closeness to challenge his phony innocence.

"Come inside with me."

It wasn't a request yet Clarissa found herself taking the hand he offered. Her steps were careful at first but the sleepiness that affected her gait had dissipated by the time they took the wide steps up to the stoop.

Eli opened the door and waved her inside. Clarissa's steps turned slow again at the discovery that they were inside his home. Subconsciously, she backed toward the door and wound up bumping against Eli instead. He squeezed her elbow; the scent of his cologne enveloped her when he bent his head close to hers.

"I said 'inside' not 'outside.'"

"I shouldn't be here." She grimaced over the sudden shortness of breath that sent her ample bustline heaving.

"Why?" he asked.

She kept her eyes on the gray marbled texture of the flooring.

Elias walked around to face Clarissa; his eyes were intent on her face. "Why shouldn't you be here?" he persisted.

Clarissa kept her head down. She knew one glance into the blue fire of his gaze would be her undoing.

"I've been inside your home, haven't I?" He was setting her back against the door. Trailing his thumb across her jaw, he then followed the move with his nose and finally his mouth.

"I've been inside your home," he murmured, adding the faintest hint of tongue to the path he charted at her jaw. "Inside your home, inside you…"

Clarissa pressed her lips together in hopes of stifling the moan demanding its freedom. "You weren't too thrilled about it last night." She took strength from someplace deep and threw the question to his side of the court.

Elias took her chin then and made her look at him. "Definitely thrilled by the fact, but not by where the fact was proven."

Her lips were barely parted when his tongue found its way between them. Clarissa wanted to slide down the door at her back, but Elias picked her up and placed her high against his broad frame. She heard her pumps clatter to the marble when her legs encircled his waist.

Elias treated himself, allowing his hands free rein over the delicious form he'd helped to awaken. They traveled across her curves as he drove his tongue hotly, wetly inside her mouth.

Clarissa could barely thrust her tongue back against his. Moans were taking over. Her stocking feet roamed his trouser legs and she rubbed herself against him in a manner that was purely wanton. Her fingertips curled into the open collar of the black denim long-sleeve shirt hanging open over a navy blue undershirt. She wanted it all gone and succeeded in brushing the shirt to the floor.

At the sound of *his* whimper, she made quick work of the undershirt, moving it up his wide torso. They broke the kiss just long enough for her to push the garment over his head.

Elias secured his hold on her bottom, cradling the fully rounded mounds neatly in his palms which eased their way beneath Clarissa's dress. He was in no hurry to take the stairs to the second level of the coolly furnished townhouse. He even halted halfway up the stairs to press her to the wall. There, his gorgeous face nuzzled into the crook of her neck. Meanwhile, his fingers worked her into a frenzy once they'd slipped past the middle of her panties.

Clarissa could feel the sudden pressure of something climactic. Elias was equally affected and he forced himself to remove his fingers before she peaked.

There was no force in the way she bumped her fists against his shoulders to relay her agitation over the move. However, her senses were once again thrumming quite nicely when he applied a deep massage to her derriere. She cupped both hands around his strong jaw and lost herself in their kiss. In seconds, it seemed she was feeling the cradle of what felt wondrously like a bed.

She wouldn't open her eyes, fearing that some aspect of her delight would end. Eli insinuated a hand between her shoulder blades and lifted her slightly to relieve her of the top of her dress. Clarissa bit down on her lip when her mouth was bereft of his.

She circled her hips when his mouth trailed every new patch of skin he uncovered during the removal of her dress. He waited until his nose was nestled between lace-covered breasts, and then added his tongue to the foreplay.

"Elias…" Her tone bordered on breathlessness. She could hardly speak, she was just that overwhelmed by his attention.

Elias had both hands beneath her back then. He unfastened the bra she wore in one fluid flick of his wrist. He caressed the soft heaving flesh protruding from the loosened cups, but had yet to fully remove the undergarment.

Instead, he tended her firming nipples through the flesh-toned lace. Weakly, Clarissa raked her fingers across the close-cut waves covering his head. Subtly, she pressed more of herself into his mouth.

The move galvanized Eli into action and he relieved her of what remained of the dress she wore. He moved on from there, getting rid of her bra, stockings and panties. He paused to survey her nude body, bracing himself against the insistent hum of his hormones which demanded to be sated.

He continued downward, spending some time nuzzling into her belly button and smirking when she wiggled in response to the tickle he planted there. He moved on then tracing the bare triangle of flesh above her sex.

Clarissa's eyes flew open when she felt his mouth on her bare inner thighs.

"Eli—"

"Shh..."

She obeyed, her every nerve ending tuned to his mouth which journeyed closer to the dip of her inner thigh until he was a breath away from the heart of her. What little strength she carried in her hands dissolved when his nose stroked her satiny intimate petals. She jerked when the tip of his tongue replaced his nose. Elias's hands firmed on her thighs and he took her in one swift powerful stroke of his tongue. Her hips lifted off the bed, but Eli was quick to settle her back down with a hand across her abdomen. Never once did he withdraw from the erotic kiss he plied her with.

Instead of rising from the bed, Clarissa rotated her hips slowly. The tension which stirred, only as a result of uncertainty for an act in which she had never indulged, gave way. Her muscles relaxed and her inner walls accommodated Eli's tongue welcomingly.

Her reaction made him groan in response and he drove his tongue deeper. Clarissa's hands rested above her head. All the while, she circled her hips and accepted all the pleasure his mouth gave. The thrusts and swirls of his tongue inside her were truly orgasm inducing. During the intense peaks of arousal, Clarissa prayed he wouldn't stop as promise of climax loomed.

To ensure that he wouldn't end his "task" too soon, she raked her hands through the silky strands of his hair and kept her hands planted there.

Elias had no intentions of stopping and placed a hand atop each of her thighs. He opened her wider to him, increasing his penetration.

Again, Clarissa lost the strength in her hands. The

only part of her still graced with the power of movement were her hips. They matched the rhythm he summoned through his shocking exploration of her body.

Elias tightened his hold on her thighs that flexed when she came hard. Moisture flooded his tongue and he groaned. The act of pleasuring her had seemed to arouse him to no end. He was rigid for her, but knew that he wouldn't take her then. This was what she should have been given that night. Slow attentiveness, not a quick slaking of lust.

Eli's heart pounded as his mind filled with ideas and images of all the things he wanted her to know with him…and only him.

"Elias…" Clarissa gasped his name and found herself overcome by the need to tremble. She gave herself to the mastery of his skills and the results they created.

Earlier, the bedroom had been doused in a golden light but when Clarissa woke from the nap she'd drifted into, once Elias had finished with her, everything was drenched in black.

She could just make out a wide door across the room. It appeared to be open and she thought she could see a thin ribbon of light there. Gingerly, she pushed up from the bed.

A search for her clothes proved fruitless once she found a lamp to assist in the looking. She didn't even see her shoes. The top sheet was practically on the floor, so she finished ripping it off the bed, wrapped it about her body and left the room.

Following the light seemed to be her best move. The long hallway outside the room was black but for the room at one end which seemed to be the source. She curled her fingers into the top of the sheet where it bunched at her breasts and headed toward an open door.

There she found Elias in what appeared to be a study. He was reclining in a worn and monstrously huge green suede armchair. Dressed in sleep pants and an ankle-length robe that was open to reveal his broad chest, he appeared quite comfortable. He rested his feet on an ottoman while studying the folder that was open across his lap.

Clarissa watched him for several moments and then she cleared her throat, bracing herself for the effect of his crystal-blue gaze meeting hers.

"My clothes?" she asked, thinking she saw the hint of a smile touch his mouth.

"They're around. Have a seat."

Clarissa selected the armchair flanking the one he occupied. It was equally worn and of a gray and burgundy plaid fabric. In spite of its hideousness, it was comfortable nonetheless.

"Why didn't you tell me?" He closed the folder, but kept his eyes downcast. When Clarissa mulled over the question a smidge longer than he felt was necessary, he fixed her with a pointed look.

"Would you have stopped?" she countered with a question of her own.

"I damn well wouldn't have had sex with you on a sofa."

"So would we have had sex at all? Or would you have just freaked out and left?"

"I don't freak out." His voice was low, monotone. "I can't say what would've happened, Clarissa, but what *wouldn't* have happened was me taking your virginity on some damn sofa."

He leaned back on the chair and rubbed at his jaw for a while. "You're better than that." His voice was low again but carried on a bit more emotion. "Your first time should have been better than that."

"Well, we can't do anything to change it now and I enjoyed it. Why can't you believe that?"

"Because you don't have anything to compare it to."

"Would you prefer that I did? That I had a hundred other guys to compare you to, Eli?"

He wouldn't answer that question. "I plan on changing that," he said instead.

"How?" She leaned forward. "By not having sex with me?"

He laughed. "What the hell do you think we just did?"

Clarissa felt her cheeks burning yet she refused to be cowed. "Is that all I can expect until you ease your guilt?"

"Guilt?" He leaned forward then, as well.

"Yes. Guilt. Because you think you treated me like I'm *easy*—something most people thought Jazmina Beaumont was."

"Jesus, you don't mince your words, do you?" He left his chair suddenly.

Clarissa had no response. She was too busy being surprised by her words, as well. She'd often made a point of *mincing* her words, figuring it was more important to listen. It was more important to accommodate others, she thought. When had she changed? Along the way, as Jaz gave her more responsibility? Or more recently when her body was awakened by the touch of Elias Joss?

"This isn't exactly about your aunt," he declared, still walking the study in a frustrated state.

"Then what?" She snuggled deeper into the chair and waited.

"Clarissa, I come from a long line of men who act first and consider the ramifications later—or never."

"Your dad," she guessed after silence had hovered for a long while.

"Father *and* grandfather." He leaned against the mantelpiece and smiled sourly.

"I've got scores of cousins to prove it. You're too good to tie yourself to a man that comes from a line like that."

She blinked owlishly and then turned on the chair in order to face him better. "Is that what we're doing, Eli? And is that what you think I expect from the man who'd been my first?"

His gaze didn't waver. "Maybe that's what the man expects."

Chapter 11

A phone's ring punctuated Elias's words. Judging by the look on his face, he was content to let it ring.

"You should get that."

"It'll keep."

"Take your call." She moved from the chair. "I'm freezing in this sheet. Take your call and I'll see you in bed."

It was a pretense, of course. His words had stunned her, yes, but more than that, they had set her upon a cloud of elation. It felt unlike anything Clarissa had ever known.

She warned herself against growing too giddy over it. But by the time she'd returned to the bedroom and snuggled into the covers, her heartbeat vibrated completely through her.

* * *

"Not a good time, Bar."

"I seem to recall *you* being the one who stood *me* up," Barker retorted none too softly. "I think I left at least six ugly messages on that damn phone of yours because of it." He laughed ill humoredly. "And why the hell aren't you answering your phone?"

"Didn't think about it."

Barker ripped out another ill-humored laugh. "Is this Elias Evan Joss I'm speaking to? 'Cause that fool never met a cell he didn't want attached to his ear."

"Clarissa's here."

"Aah…'nuff said."

"So will you accept my apology about missing our lunch date at Hemming's?"

"Not without a lot of pleading, but since you answered your home phone, do you mind taking a few minutes away from the lovely Miss David to tell me what was so important earlier?"

"Do you know who Cleve Echols's investors are?"

The unexpected question did render Barker speechless for a time.

"Do I take that as a yes or a no?" Eli sat on the edge of his desk and looked down at the page next to him. "If it's a 'no' then I've got a list of names here if you'd like to see them?"

"How?" Barker's voice came through the line at last.

"Des. Never underestimate the power of a prime executive assistant," Eli mused.

"I got a list of my own."

"Right. So do you want to get together and compare notes or are *your* notes off-limits?"

"What else did Des find?" Barker asked instead.

"Just the names." Eli looked down at the list again. "But he did recognize two of them—one he was sure you'd know. Liesel Hertz? She's an anchor at WPXI, right?" Eli referenced the name of Barker's employer. "What's goin' on, Bar?" he continued when silence met his question.

"Hell, Eli, I don't know."

"Well, what do you *think* you know?"

"At first it looked like nothing," Barker finally shared. "There's nothing wrong with folks going in to invest money."

"Except?" Elias prompted.

"*Except*...the money invested was substantial. Liesel and her husband don't make anywhere near the amounts I knew were being funneled into the Echols's project."

Eli turned his back on the list and frowned. "How do you know how much was being invested?"

"Never underestimate the power of a prime executive assistant, right?" Barker returned Eli's earlier remark.

"That doesn't mean your coworker and her hubby couldn't afford to invest that money. You don't know what they could have stashed away."

"Yeah..."

"Des said the names he recognized from Philadelphia were real movers and shakers around the city. Like Melanie Shales, she—"

"Who?"

"Shales, Melanie. Surely a woman like that and the rest would have that kind of money."

"Maybe..." Barker's tone was unquestionably distracted.

"What is it, Bar?"

"Not sure...something...listen, are you gonna stand me up again if I ask to meet and discuss this list of yours?"

"No. And will you tell me what's on your mind?"

Barker didn't try to hide his groan. "I only pray I'm wrong."

The men ended their conversation and then Eli shut down the lights on his way out of the study and back to the bedroom to Clarissa. He stopped just short of clearing the door when he felt his heart take a weird beat as he recalled the last thing he'd said to her.

No words that even hinted at commitment had ever entered a conversation between him and *any* woman. However, Clarissa David in a very short span of time had proven that she was more than *any* woman. She had given him pause from the moment she had glided into Stanford Crothers's shop. She could mystify him without doing a damn thing, he thought. How was that possible? Women had done all manner of things to grab his attention. The attempts had worn thin in short order. Eli had come to recognize all the ploys—all but the act of doing absolutely nothing.

So now what? he asked himself while making his way down the hall. Again, he considered what he'd said to Clarissa about "tying" himself to her. God help him, he meant it and it terrified him. It was not because he wasn't ready and that was a shock in and of itself. No, *tying* himself to her meant she was *tying* herself to him, as well.

Could he do right by her? Would he? She was too special a woman to have anything less than the best kind of man.

Elias opened the bedroom door slowly so as not to awaken her if she was already sleeping. He didn't call her name but took off his robe and slipped between the covers next to her.

She had dozed off, but not very deeply and snuggled back into him when she felt his body behind hers. Eli could just hear her voice, whisper soft as she spoke his name amid her light slumber.

He hid his face in the crook of her neck and breathed in her scent. Clarissa woke slowly, blinking until her eyes had adjusted to the dark.

"Eli?"

"Shh...back to sleep."

She refused and turned on her side toward him. Boldly, she instigated a kiss that grew progressively hot until Elias stopped her.

"You should rest." He spoke the advice with great effort.

Clarissa was in no mood to oblige. "It's your turn," she said against his mouth before her tongue outlined its shape. She shivered at the feel of his goatee whiskers beneath her nails.

Eli didn't need much coaxing to see her side of things. A sound loomed deep in his throat and he grabbed her tight, lifting her over him. Never breaking the kiss, he kneaded and squeezed her derriere. The generous mound of flesh that filled his hands was indeed a sharp stimulator.

Keeping his hold intact, Elias manipulated Clarissa's

moves, driving her into the ever-stiffening erection beneath his sleep pants. One leg raised at the knee provided a deeper cradle for her nude body. She virtually
melted into him.

Tentatively, her hand smoothed the flawless wall of
his muscular chest. Her hips moved in a timeless erotic
manner which required no manipulation from Elias.

Clarissa broke their kiss in order to trail her mouth
down his neck. She was fascinated and tingly anew
as her lips brushed the powerful cords beneath his
caramel-colored skin. Lower, they ventured across the
pectorals that flexed in response to her mouth's caress.

She moved onward, tasting him when her tongue
flicked across his nipples and then down to outline the
array of muscles that somehow seemed carved into his
abdomen.

Elias grunted when he felt her tongue encircling his
navel, but the gesture wasn't out of arousal. Well...not
entirely. He squeezed Clarissa's upper arms and managed to draw her away only slightly. "No." His voice
was hushed.

"Why?" Her tone was equally hushed in the dark-
ness. "I only want to repay your attentiveness," she
teased sweetly.

"You don't have to."

"I want to." She let her words relay the smile on her
face, but gasped suddenly when his hold on her arms
tightened to an almost painful state.

"No," he insisted.

"Eli—" She didn't have the time for further arguments. He assumed control then, flipping her on her
back and kissing her harshly.

Clarissa welcomed it; almost instantly she forgot her arguments as pleasure stabbed her from all angles. Her moans and whispers of delight threw Elias's hormones into overdrive. His mouth was at work over her body while he freed himself. The fine material of the sleep pants was nothing but an irritant next to his rigid arousal. Blindly, he groped in and around the night table until he had located a condom.

Clarissa felt tears pressuring her eyes as a result of the exquisite sensations he stirred. Eli rose above, plundering her with his index and middle fingers while his thumb stimulated her clit with slow mind-numbing rotations. As Clarissa tumbled into an erotic abyss, he used his perfect teeth to rip into the condom packet he'd located. Clarissa let her eyes drift shut, biting her lip as faint orgasmic waves began to crest from his actions. Her lashes fluttered when he suddenly withdrew his fingers.

Clarissa didn't have the chance for questions. His fingers were replaced by the incomparable fullness of his erection delving long and breathtakingly deep inside her. She pressed her head into the pillows and opened her mouth while satisfaction circulated in her veins.

No sound emerged from her lips. She would have wrapped her legs around his back, but he kept a wide hand across her thigh and prevented movement on her part.

Clarissa clutched his powerful forearms and pleaded without knowing what she pleaded for. Seconds passed and then she was peaking again, coming hard as the climax overtook her.

Eli covered her and gave into the thunderous waves

of need that demanded that he take her fiercely and selfishly. His thrusts took on a rapacious intensity that brought him to eruption almost in tandem to Clarissa's orgasm.

The lovers drifted into a satiated lounge. Their mingled breathing filled the room with sound for long moments.

"Would I scare you if I told you that I wanted to keep you here—right here—just like this?" he asked while his handsome face was still hidden in her neck.

"Hmm—" she included a chuckle "—that'd make for some pretty awkward meetings with Linus and Tigo."

"In that case—" Eli groaned after they'd laughed a while "—I better take what I can get while I have you."

"And how long will that be?"

He raised his head. "*You* tell *me*."

Clarissa was opening her mouth to try, but only released a cry when she felt him stiffen inside her.

Elias shook his head. "Tell me later."

Clarissa arrived, lovely yet slightly disheveled, for her 11:00 a.m. meeting at the club.

"Mmm...someone's glowing," Monesha Baker teased.

"Nothing like a good night's sleep." Clarissa pulled her tote strap from her shoulder.

"Oh, I doubt that." Monesha's meaning was clear.

"Don't give me a hard time, all right," Clarissa playfully begged. Guessing what the suggestive follow-up would be to *that* response, she raised a warning finger. "Save it, Mo. Has my eleven o'clock been waiting long?"

"Not so long that *you'll* look bad for being ten minutes late."

"Thanks, Mo," Clarissa sang while hurrying down the short corridor to the office.

"I'm so sorry for being late," Clarissa was saying after introducing herself to Leta Fields of the Breck Humanitarian Committee.

"No apology needed." Leta's broad welcoming smile was mirrored in her voice. "I had the chance to take a look at the club and chat with a few of the girls."

"Well, then." Clarissa set down her tote while smoothing a hand across her rust-colored, split-front skirt. "Are you here to tell me that my aunt's out of the running for the award?"

"Heavens no!" Leta's laughter was genuine. "Not at all. Those young women out there made it clear that Jazmina Beaumont offered a place for them that was a beginning instead of the end of the line."

Clarissa pushed her hands into the skirt's pockets and studied Leta with greater interest.

"They couldn't stop talking about how much they owed her for caring." Leta propped a hand to her dented chin and considered. "I'd love to have a few of them speak at the awards dinner."

Clarissa felt a slight pressure behind her eyes and blinked before the happy tears showed themselves. "Thank you for coming to tell me in person."

"Well, that's not the only reason that I'm here." Leta's slightly bugged eyes appeared a smidgeon enlarged. She leaned in as though she were about to share a secret. "Have you heard of the Reed House Jazz Supper?"

"Well, yes, Aunt Jaz and I were—" The memory suddenly unleashed the tears she was trying to hide. "I'm sorry."

"Oh, Clarissa, no." Leta dropped a reassuring arm around Clarissa's shaking shoulders and squeezed. "I was so sorry to hear of Jazmina's passing." She bowed her head and patted Clarissa's shoulder for a time. "I hope it won't be callous of me to ask you to attend the supper anyway, dear?"

At Clarissa's brief nod, Leta continued. "Each year, in addition to the Humanitarian award, the committee selects a local charity to acknowledge for its efforts. We always ask the Humanitarian award recipient to do the ceremonial presenting of the acknowledgment check." She turned to look at Clarissa more directly.

"I apologize for the late notice but with everything that's happened…we understand if you're not up to presenting the check in your aunt's place."

"No, Leta." Clarissa was already shaking her head. "I'd be honored—really. Thank you for this." She took both the woman's hands in hers. "Thanks for helping to give my aunt's name a proud meaning in this town."

The bracelet Leta wore dangled beneath the cuff of her blouse when she shook Clarissa's hand. "This would've happened anyway. Jazmina did far too much good for it to never come to light." She patted Clarissa's shoulder.

"If you're up for it we can speak soon about the particulars, all right?"

"Oh, yes. Yes, of course." Clarissa smiled and watched as Leta turned to file though the papers inside the case she'd arrived with. While the woman was occupied, Clarissa cherished a moment to remember her aunt.

Elias shook hands with the three men who made up the architectural firm of Rosen, Bergen and Finley and then he waved them on ahead into his office before turning to his partners who lagged behind.

"Sorry for the late notice, man," said Linus who had arranged the meeting. "This was the only other day we could get you four together." He nodded at the architects who were getting settled at the square conference table in Eli's office.

"We tried reaching you on your cell all day yesterday. Where the hell were you?" Tigo asked.

"Around." Eli shrugged.

"Well, did you lose your phone somewhere?" Linus frowned suspiciously while tapping the toe of his black wing tips. "That's the only reason you wouldn't have the damn thing plastered to your ear."

"Correction, man." Tigo slapped Linus's shoulder. "That's not the *only* reason with the enticing Ms. David in the picture."

"Aah…" Linus slanting gaze twinkled with devilment.

"Thanks to you both for remembering the person we're supposed to be working for." Elias motioned toward his office. "Can we get on with this?"

"Hold up." Linus suddenly shifted a stunned look to Tigo and then back to Eli. "That *is* why we couldn't get you. You were with her all afternoon?"

"We're not doin' this…" Eli groaned.

"Man, what? That's good to hear." Tigo kept his voice hushed, but his excitement was clear.

"You're finally livin' more than workin'." Linus's mouth curled to attest how impressed he was.

Tigo pressed a hand to his heart in a show of emotion. "We're proud of you, kid."

Elias bowed his head, but couldn't hide his smile. "Can we go back to work now?" he pleaded finally.

Linus and Tigo slapped their partner's back and then urged him to precede them.

"This is gonna confuse a lot of people, 'specially the girls." Rayelle's face was a picture of awe.

"I know." Clarissa gave a hasty wave and then she sat close to her friend on the love seat in the manager's office. "But I really think they'll be excited by the possibilities."

"Of what?" Ray blinked, unimpressed. "Clay, all those girls didn't grow up with aspirations of being prima ballerinas. Jaz thought they could do anything, but the truth is that most of them have no intentions of doing anything other than finding a sugar daddy or a rich, stupid hubby to take care of 'em."

"I've talked to people who knew she wanted this."

"And I don't doubt that. Miss Jaz was always talkin' about the changes she wanted to make around here. She wanted to make the place better. That's where the whole remodeling idea came from."

Clarissa leaned back on the mosaic-print love seat. "So why don't you seem as on board with this as I'd expect?"

"Clay, Miss J didn't want this for you." Ray crossed

her legs beneath the hem of her gold pencil-slim skirt and sighed. "Honey, she didn't want you makin' a career out of this. She knew *she* wasn't goin' anywhere as long as she was alive and runnin' things. Don't you see? That's why she left you the club. She wanted you to get out and make your own way somewhere. If the club couldn't become what Miss J wanted, she'd have rather it be nothing at all. I had instructions for taking care of the girls should that happen."

"I want to do this for her, Ray." Clarissa's voice teetered on the edge of belligerence. "We'll make sure the girls not interested are taken care of."

Ray blinked and straightened where she sat. "You're serious, aren't you? Have you talked to Mr. Cole about it?"

Clarissa picked something invisible from her skirt. "I'll get around to it. I'd like to have more details in place before I go to him. It's the only way he'll take me seriously." Her velvety brown eyes narrowed in Ray's direction. "Seems like a good idea considering how hard it is to convince my best friend."

Ray shrugged, but joined in when Clarissa laughed.

"Thanks for rearranging to meet us today, guys," Eli said as he shook hands with the architects.

"We'd love it if you could work in a visit to each of the sites, man," Daren Finley was saying.

Edward Rosen nodded at his partner's suggestion. "Viewing the work in phases will keep everyone on the same page."

"I agree." Eli stroked his goatee. "Let me see what I can work into my schedule."

The men shook hands again and then Tigo and Linus offered to escort the architects out when Eli's phone rang.

"When can we get together to look at this list of yours?" Barker asked before Eli finished saying "hello."

"Whenever you're ready to level with me," Eli bartered.

"All right then, tell me how you like this. Our fellow Philadelphians on that list have something else in common besides their gender."

Eli tugged his tie loose. "You gonna make me guess?"

Barker had no such intentions. "They've all got cops for husbands," he said.

Chapter 12

"Eli?" Clarissa called as she knocked on the open door and stuck her head just inside the office. His assistant was gone so she hesitantly made her way inside the room.

"Elias…" she called again but didn't really expect him to answer.

For a time, she admired the room and its stunning view of downtown. Moving on, Clarissa approached the shelving and the photos of Eli with his friends and family. Correction—his friends and his mother. She noticed that there was no sign of any photos of Eli's father. That was understandable. Nevertheless, Clarissa couldn't help but think over what that meant and how her aunt was to blame for it.

The knock on the door kept her thoughts from running off too far. Clarissa saw Elias leaning on the wall just inside the room. Hastily, she replaced the photo she'd taken from the wall.

"Desmond wasn't at his desk...you asked me to come over." She saw fit to remind him when he only watched her silently.

As she spoke, Eli was shortening the distance between them. Then he was kissing her in the way he'd perfected to wipe her mind clear of almost everything except registering his touch.

"I guess you're okay with me being here." Every part of her hummed.

"I'm very okay with it." He bent to brush his nose across her earlobe.

"I, um...I got the feeling this was about business when you called."

"Did you?" He was more interested in nuzzling her ear and fingering her clipped hair then.

Clarissa was working her hands up along the crisp dark fabric of the shirt he'd worn that day. An olive-green tie with flecks of a darker green hung loose about his collar. Her intention was to tug it free. He got serious then.

"The architects want us to come out and visit some of the sites." The beckoning blue of his gaze followed the flip of her hair when he twirled it around his fingers. "They want us to see the work while it's in progress. Make sure we're all on the same page."

Clarissa's voluminous eyes followed the movement of her hand on the tie. "Are all the decisions, um...is everything finalized now?"

"Pretty much." Curious, he bent his knees just

slightly to bring himself more level with her gaze. "They've got the plans done. What's up?"

She shook her head quickly. His finger beneath her chin stifled the movement. "What is it?"

"I—"

"Tell me the truth."

She grimaced at his prediction that she'd lie. "Is it too late to scrap the plans? I'm thinking of going in a different direction but it's still way up in the air." She inhaled as though the words had consumed her.

"We can do whatever you want."

"But not without a lot of problems, right?"

"Did you hear me?" He braced his index finger along her jaw and encouraged her head up. "Whatever you want. Understood?" He waited on her nod and smiled when she complied.

"We should arrange another sit-down with the architects before any trips are planned. You'll need to be there, give us your ideas—no holding back, okay?"

She nodded, eased by the weight of worrying being lifted. "'Kay," she whispered a millisecond before his tongue reengaged hers.

They were in the depths of a lusty splendid kiss when a knock on the open office door turned their attention to Desmond. Clarissa bowed her head and smiled when a frustrated groan rumbled in Eli's chest.

"Sorry, boss," Desmond whispered when Elias met him at the door.

"You can make it up by takin' off for the day."

"No problem." Desmond grinned in the face of the grimly delivered instruction. "Just wanted to drop off the info you asked for on those names."

"Anything good?" Eli took the folder.

"It's not complete but I was able to get full location material."

"Get out of here." Eli dismissed his assistant and closed the door on Desmond's still-grinning face. At his desk, he dropped the file to the desk as an afterthought.

More interested in picking up where he left off with Clarissa, he hauled her curvy body high and subjected her to more kissing and caressing.

The buzzing phone interrupted them that time. Eli was content to let it buzz.

"Could be the architects."

"It's not."

Clarissa laughed at the agitated growl of his voice. "Sooner you answer, sooner you can get back." She spoke through their kiss, giggling when he grumbled and went to take care of the call.

"Don't you even do it," he ordered when she made a move to straighten her clothes.

Elias went to snatch up the phone. When he handled the call, Clarissa studied the baseball paperweight on the desk. The file from Desmond had fallen open next to it. Clarissa studied the contents idly while she fidgeted with the paperweight.

"Sorry about that. What?" Eli noticed the strange smile she wore.

"It's funny." She shrugged.

"What?"

Clarissa glanced toward the open folder. "All these people live in cities where there are Jazzy B's. Are we meeting with them when we head out?"

Elias spent little time focusing on the file. His attention and gaze was being held captive by the line of Clarissa's thigh visible behind the front split in her skirt.

"It's something Des is working on. Will you let me take you out to dinner?" he asked in the same breath.

"I'm supposed to meet Ray." She leaned over the desk to tug his tie. "We don't have plans for dessert, though."

He cuffed her neck in his hand. "Cake or ice cream?"

"Surprise me."

More kissing was a given following the exchange. Clarissa was in no hurry to bring an end to it, but Eli knew he'd have her on the desk in nothing flat if he didn't.

"I'll see you later," he promised and dropped a short simple peck to her kiss-swollen lips. He released her, watching while she grabbed her stuff and waved before disappearing through the door.

Alone, Elias turned his focus back to the open folder.

"Ms. Keats, we're so sorry. This is very embarrassing but the table isn't ready just yet." The hostess for the Grill Moon was clutching and releasing her hands so tightly they were almost as red as her hair.

"It's fine," Rayelle promised and lifted the portfolio she carried. "I've got plenty to read until my *date* gets here." She referred to Clarissa.

The young redhead still appeared uncertain. "The bar's practically full and I hate to ask you to stand here when this is *our* fault." She bit her lip and gazed frantically about the packed lobby and bar. "Just one sec, Ms. Keats," she said suddenly and speed walked into the mesh of bodies. She made a beeline for the gentleman who appeared to be the only occupant at the small round table for two.

"Excuse me, Mr. G?"

Barker Grant looked up from the work he'd brought in. "What's up, Holly?"

"I'm so sorry about this, Mr. G, but would you mind sharing your table with a lady until we have her ready to be seated in the dining room?"

"Is the lady cute?"

Holly blinked more profusely when she smiled. "Most of the waiters think she's beyond it."

"Well, then, what are you waiting for?" Barker pushed aside his work. He watched Holly wave until she'd caught the eye of the tall honey-toned beauty near the front of the crowded space.

"Barker Grant, this is Ms. Rayelle Keats."

Barker motioned toward the empty chair at the table. "Ms. Keats."

"Rayelle, please," she urged once Holly had walked off. She tucked her portfolio into her lap and appeared exasperated. "I'm sorry about this."

"I don't know why. Holly just made my day."

Rayelle smiled, instantly at ease around the dark intense-looking man. "My girlfriend shouldn't be long."

Barker rarely smiled but, when he did, the effect on his already appealing features was truly flattering. "Is she the jealous type?"

Caught off guard by the query, Rayelle broke into a wave of laughter that actually made her eyes tear. "It's business," she was finally able to explain. "Maybe I should have referred to her as my best friend."

Barker pretended to cringe. "And how well do best friends mix with business?"

Ray shrugged and caused the gold herringbone necklace to glint against the light. "So far, so good," she said.

Barker studied Rayelle closely for a while and it was obvious that he enjoyed what he saw. Soon though, his gaze shifted and he offered a slight nod. "Looks like our time's up."

Ray turned in her seat and saw Clarissa near the front of the bar along with the waving hostess. Sighing, she turned back to Barker. "Thanks for sharing your table."

"I'll have to give Holly a very good tip for this."

"Good night." Ray spoke through more laughter.

"Are you sure about this, Clay?" Ray was asking some ten minutes later while she and Clarissa enjoyed appetizers at their booth.

Clarissa was thumbing through Jazmina's mysterious notebook and paying little if any attention to the potato skins Rayelle was massacring.

"I'm as sure of this as I am of the fact that you're a little pissed that I interrupted your chat earlier," Clarissa said.

Ray appeared stumped for only a moment and then she kicked a heel on Clarissa's boot where her legs were crossed under the table. "It wasn't even like that."

"Yet."

"Anyway." Ray shook her hair out of her face. "Are you sure about involving the police in this? I mean, are you even certain something illegal's going on?"

"I think that Sophie can tell us that and she's the only one I agreed to draw into this. Besides—" Clarissa set down the notebook and folded her hands atop it "—Aunt Jaz was already talking to her about this anyway. Something had her on edge and she was pretty sure it was something fishy about this book." She tapped a round French-tipped nail to the cover. "Can't hurt to let her have a look at it and tell us if we're wrong."

"And what happens if we *aren't* wrong?" Ray folded her arms across the draping neckline of her charcoal-brown sweater. "Have you thought about what that would mean and who'd be affected most by it?"

"I won't let anything happen to the girls, Ray."

"I'm not talking about the girls, Clay." Ray's gaze dropped briefly to the notebook. "If Miss Jaz figured out something, why wouldn't she find someone to bounce her suspicions off of *before* going to the cops?"

"Waymon Cole?" Clarissa spoke the man's name in a hooked manner. "Ray, are you saying—"

"I'm only asking if you've looked at this from all directions." Rayelle cast a quick glance over her shoulder. "If something shady was going on, Miss Jaz would have only kept it quiet from those closest to her for a couple reasons. Either she didn't think there was any reason to get them upset or there was someone she couldn't trust."

"Good timing." Barker laughed into his phone's tiny receiver. "I was just about to call and ask if we could meet."

"Had I known I'd be free tonight, I would have suggested it." Elias's voice came through the line.

"Yeah, I saw your girl having dinner. Her dinner date's way more incredible looking than you are, kid."

"Humph, I'm surprised you haven't already introduced yourself to Ray."

"Aah…so you already knew about her dinner plans?" Barker sounded impressed. "Is it like that now? You guys keeping each other in the loop about every move you make?"

"What can I say?" Eli conceded.

"Is it serious?"

"I want it to be." Eli followed the admission with an agitated groan as if the words had floored him. "Am I crazy?"

Barker chuckled. "Certifiable."

"Then what I'm about to say next won't sound too out of place."

"Shoot."

"If all the women on this list have cops for husbands, all live in towns where there are Jazzy B's *and* all are Cleve Echols's investors who for some unknown reason decided to hitch their sails to Waymon Cole's ship, what the hell kind of weird connection does all that suggest?"

Barker was undeniably suspicious. His voice of reason told him that something was amiss. As it was the voice that he often hated listening to, he guessed the *suggestion* was that all Elias's connections added up to something pretty ugly.

"Do you think Clarissa knows anything?" Barker asked.

"I doubt it," Eli said after a beat. "I get the feeling Jaz Beaumont tried to keep her niece out of the loop on things that had the potential to make her look bad.

Last thing she needs is *me* of all people coming to her with any more negatives about the woman."

"Even if the negatives are founded?"

Eli's responding sigh was mixed with a more guttural sound. "If it's founded, that spells a bigger problem, especially for Clarissa."

"It'd mean her aunt was a criminal, E."

"On top of everything else."

"We'll figure it out, man." Barker didn't need to be face-to-face with Eli to know that the man was beyond tense. "I'm on it, all right?"

"I hear you. Look, I'm gonna let you go, okay?"

"What the hell…?" Barker murmured spotting Detective Sophia Hail shaking hands with Clarissa and Rayelle.

"Bar? What's up?" Eli was asking over the phone.

"Not sure. Sophie Hail's here about to sit down with your girl."

"Official capacity?"

"Hard to say."

"Could be a girl's night," Eli reasoned.

"What was it you were saying about weird connections?"

"Right…so what's one more?"

"Right." Barker's trademark scowl had returned.

"I need somethin' concrete before I go to Cleve Echols, Bar. Before this stuff affects Clarissa."

"I need whatever you have on this, E."

"Sending it now."

The call ended and Barker paid his check. He spent a few additional minutes watching the three women talking intensely before he left.

* * *

Later that night, Clarissa was back at Jazmina's house and on the phone with event planner Dave Blackmon. The topic of their discussion was a dinner party she wanted to have before the Humanitarian gathering for her aunt.

"This a celebration dinner for the award?" Dave was asking.

"No, nothing related to that, just something I want to do for the girls."

The doorbell rang and Eli's name registered in Clarissa's head. She headed down from her bedroom, recalling their plans for coffee and dessert. She was still going back and forth with Dave over the particulars for the proposed event, when she pulled open the front door.

Elias's expression changed to one of sensual shock, his blue stare charting a repetitive path along the length of her. Clarissa paid little attention to his approval. She pulled him across the threshold, brushed her lips over his jaw and continued her discussion with Dave.

Elias, meanwhile, was still surveying her attire. The chemise-styled gown just brushed her midthigh. Although she wore an ankle-length chiffon robe with it, the garment only enhanced the appeal of her barely there nightie.

"I've got some things I want to discuss with the girls...newer directions for the club." Clarissa was still focused on the phone conversation and not on how closely Eli trailed her as they took the stairs back to the second floor.

"I'm trying to get their opinion on my ideas and I want to keep the night flowing with food and drinks."

Dave chuckled over the phone line. "Clarissa, Clarissa…are you tryin' to bribe your employees?"

"Dave…" She laughed. "You know me, 'course I am."

Elias had been following Clarissa up the staircase like an obedient puppy. He blinked as though waking from a heavy sleep when he heard her addressing Dave. He paused at the door of the bedroom suite she occupied instead of following her inside.

There he took time to observe the room and how her presence seemed to cling to it. His focus however was quickly returned to Clarissa when she sat in an armchair and began to lotion her legs. He waited until she'd finished the task and then he crossed the room and pulled her from the chair.

Claiming her spot, Eli tugged her down to straddle his lap. He pulled the tie on the chemise nightie and, loosening the bodice, allowed her breasts to protrude a bit more from the opening.

Clarissa's voice went faint in the middle of her phone discussion. "Dave? Let me get back to you, all right?"

"Dave?" Elias questioned when the call ended. His nose outlined the lush fragrant flesh that bubbled past the lacy chemise.

Clarissa was at once overwrought by his touch. When he gave a warning squeeze to her thigh, she recalled his question.

"He's a, um…party, event planner…I wanted to have a dinner here at the house for the girls—mmm…" She cherished the stroke of his thumb across a nipple that appeared half in, half out of the bodice. "Wanted to talk to them about changes…at the club."

"Nice of you…" Eli had already retasked his focus to the sensitive flesh below her earlobe. At the same time, his hands slid beneath the hem of the gown until he was cradling her bottom in his wide palms. He worked her into his groin and the stiff proof of his arousal.

They kissed until Clarissa's incessant gasping in response to his fondling prevented her from fully taking part in the duel between their tongues.

Elias chuckled arrogantly over her response and thrust his tongue deep into her open mouth. Intermittently, he raked his tongue across her teeth and outlined her lips. He was attacked by a groan when she started to rotate her hips which caused his erection to throb in a mixture of pleasure and pain.

Clarissa finished undoing the ties of her chemise gown. She'd barely parted the material when Eli's gorgeous face was hidden in the almond-brown swells of her bosom.

His hand left her butt to grope a breast while he luxuriated in the satin feel of the other by grazing his whisker-roughened cheek along it. Clarissa was concentrating on opening the denim shirt he wore outside cream-colored jeans. Desperation to see his awesome chest fueled her actions.

Eli was suckling madly on the breast he held. Clarissa was pulling apart his shirt and going to work on his jean fastening. His hand tightened again on her derriere and she knew that he meant to carry her to the bed.

In silent refusal, Clarissa closed her hands tight over the chair arms and resisted the move. She initiated the next kiss while freeing him from his jeans and boxer shorts. Once she held him and began to work her hand along the rigid length of his shaft, Eli seemed to melt into the chair.

"Please, Clari."

She felt her confidence grow over his tortured request. He didn't ask her to stop and she had no intention of doing so. Leaning back again, she used her free hand to take a condom packet from her robe. Raising it to her mouth, she ripped into the casing.

Eli's sex flared against her palm in response and anticipation. Clarissa moved again, to tease his sleek chest with faint grazes from her nipples. She began to suckle his earlobe while setting their protection in place.

Clarissa had barely completed the task when Elias took her hips captive and settled her down with an aching sweetness. She let her head fall back while Eli moved forward to feast on her breasts. All the while, he directed her moves. Clarissa held on to the chair arms and she was on the verge of orgasm less than a minute later.

It was her turn to please then. She'd wanted to maintain control that time. She might have been a virgin, but she wasn't completely clueless. She wanted to please him as he had her and was more than a little eager to prove that she could.

"This was for you…" She moaned while absorbing the sensation his deep penetration stirred within her. "*I* wanted to please *you*." She heard Eli laugh then and she frowned slightly in irritation even as she gasped over his manipulation of her body.

Eli's laughter sounded rather faint but it was definitely humor filled. "You are without a doubt pleasing me, Clari."

She was breathless. "You aren't letting me do any-thing…"

"Are you serious?" The blue-green of his stare sharpened a bit when he winced. Pleasure was lancing through him at a relentless pace. The feel of it made him rest his head back on the chair and watch her in helpless wonder.

"Do you feel that?" he managed to ask.

"Yes…"

"Do you know what that is?" He gave her a "punish-ing" thrust when she didn't answer fast enough.

"That's you, Eli." She bit her lip.

"And how do I feel, Clarissa? How do I feel inside you?"

"Mmm…"

"Answer me…"

"Mmm…stiff…hard…good…"

"Look at me." He waited for her to comply. "You do that. You do that to me every time I see you. Every time…" The words carried on a whisper seconds before they indulged in another kiss.

Chapter 13

"Don't even think I forgot about it." Clarissa's words slurred. She tried and failed to keep her eyes open while accusing Elias of taking her mind off the dessert he had promised her last night.

Eli chuckled while nuzzling his face into the preferred resting spot on her chest. "You're a hard woman to please. How about dinner tonight?"

"I only asked for dessert."

"You should know by now how much I hate doing things half-assed."

"Dinner it is. Will you cook?"

"Just be ready by seven."

The couple cherished the act of simple lounging and caressing. Moments passed in an unhurried blur until the unique sound of a vibrating phone filled the air.

Clarissa sighed irritably. "When do you have to go?"

"You have a lot to learn about being a boss." Eli grinned and flipped Clarissa to her back. "I go when I want."

"You speak like a boss who doesn't run a club," she told him when he let her up for air following a thorough kiss. "Running a club is a whole different world. *Literally.*"

The last word captured Eli's attention and he cocked his head. "Does this have anything to do with these changes you're talking about?"

"Jaz wanted out of the strip club business."

"She was retiring?"

Clarissa shook her head over Eli's guess. "Wanted to turn the place into a dance studio."

"What?" His expression was a melding of disbelief and amusement. "Are you considering that?"

"Depends on the girls."

"And Waymon Cole." Eli frowned at Clarissa's nonchalant shrug. "He was your aunt's business manager."

"The club belongs to me and I'm loyal only to the girls."

"Who've you told about this?"

"Just Ray, and the girls will know soon."

Eli nodded. "Keep it that way, all right?"

The warning roused Clarissa's suspicions but she had no chance to question him. The phone was buzzing again. Elias took the call. Clarissa snuggled into the covers, but studied him curiously when he groaned over whatever the caller had to say before he hung up.

She was of a mind to question his vague comment regarding her upcoming talk with the dancers, but her intentions were thwarted. When she opened her mouth, he filled it with his tongue. All too soon however, he was telling her that he had to go.

"No...stay..."

As if to appease her, Eli kissed his way down her body, spending considerable time where she yearned most for him. He left her unsated, though.

"Be ready by seven." He spoke the words into her inner thigh and then left the bed.

Clarissa responded by aiming a pillow and throwing it dead center against his back.

"Couldn't this wait?" Eli's caramel-kissed features were contorted into a full-blown glare.

"We thought you'd like knowing how your money's being spent." Linus swiveled his desk chair that matched the walnut-brown trousers he wore. "But if not, me and Tigo have no problems cookin' the books and runnin' off to Tahiti."

Eli grunted a laugh and massaged his thumb into a patch of skin between his sleek brows. "I always had a feelin' about you two."

"Come on, man, be serious. We're tryin' to give you some kind of hint," Tigo said while pushing up the sleeves of a black crew shirt.

Eli cleared his throat and waited.

"You've been very un-workaholic-like lately," Linus noted.

Tigo followed with a solemn nod. "Probably don't even know where your phone is."

Pacing Linus's office, Eli smoothed both hands across the dark close-cut waves covering his head.

"You fallin' for her, Eli?"

"Very hard," Eli replied to Tigo's question without hesitation. "I haven't even known her that long."

Linus and Tigo exchanged looks. Tigo's inquiry had been intentionally vague yet Eli's quick response told both men that their partner had only one thing—one woman—on his mind.

"We're gonna have to arrange a new meeting with the architects before we can start making the trips out to the sites." Eli took a seat on the arm of a cream-colored leather sofa near the door. "Clarissa's got some things she needs to discuss with them. Can't wait."

"Not a problem," Tigo said. "They aren't set to leave town for another few days."

"All right then," Eli bowed his head to stroke his goatee for a few seconds. He then tugged his shirt cuffs and stood. "Can we finish this later? Got some calls to make."

"No prob." Linus waved, and then grinned at Tigo when the door closed at Eli's back.

"Damn fool's in love," Tigo said.

Linus could only chuckle.

"Do you think the girls will be on board with this? Last thing I need is to have their worlds turned upside down." Clarissa raked her fingers through her glossy cropped hair and then held her head in her hands.

Rayelle idly stirred her coffee. "I think there's a good chance for success, Clay. I mean, a lot of the girls that come here do have aspirations of being serious dancers. That business though…" She sighed. "It's a tough one to break into."

"This is gonna hit their pocketbooks pretty hard. Some harder than others maybe."

Rayelle knew what Clarissa was referring to. "There's a chance that none of them had any involvement in that."

"Still…" Clarissa pushed back from the table. "Aren't many *big* tips exchanging hands at a dance studio. That is, if the cops don't shut the whole place down."

"There's a chance Sophie won't find anything."

"Do you really believe that?"

Ray blew a tuft of hair from her eyes. "So what are we gonna do?"

"Make the changes that Jaz wanted."

"And the consequences?"

"We'll worry about them when, *if* the time comes."

"Impressive." Ray's neat line of brows raised a notch. "Could a certain turquoise-eyed brotha have anything to do with your…laid-back attitude?"

Clarissa merely shrugged and wrapped herself tighter into the black linen robe she wore. Her easy expression harbored an all-too-concerned tinge moments later.

"Ray, I've questioned and second-guessed myself more in the last two weeks than I ever have in my life."

"Understandable." Ray tapped her spoon to the cup absently. "Especially when you've spent your entire life doing what others expect of you. You're finally living and that's what Jaz wanted."

"Yeah…" Clarissa toyed with a sheaf of paper napkins at the breakfast nook. "I don't know if she meant for it to go this fast—*this* soon."

"Only thing that matters is how it feels. How *does* it feel?"

Clarissa stretched out her arms across the table. "I'd say 'phenomenal' but who am I to know what phenomenal feels like?"

Rayelle lifted her coffee cup as if to toast. "Trust me, Clay. A woman knows when she's feeling phenomenal."

"Will I sound like a total idiot of I said it was scary?"

Ray set down the cup and leaned in as if she were about to share a secret. "Clarissa Alicia David—are you in love with that man?"

"All of 'em? You're sure?" Eli was asking when he and Barker met to discuss what had turned up in the investigation of the names.

"Sure as I can be." Barker massaged his forearm below the rolled sleeve of his cobalt-blue shirt. "These women are all married to cops and all live in towns where there are Jazzy B's clubs."

"I'll be damned...."

Barker observed his friend with a wary eye. "E, man...I gotta ask if your guess could be off here? Maybe you're tryin' to tie this together because of that old drama."

Elias raised his hands and then laid them flat on the table they shared. "I'm not. I swear it's not that. I just have it in my head that it's too much coincidence with Cole's involvement." For emphasis, Eli braced his elbows to the table and cradled his head in his hands.

"You say anything to Clarissa yet?"

"Humph." Eli let Barker see the slyness in his gaze. "We don't spend much time talkin' business."

"Right." Barker closed his eyes and grinned. "She doesn't spend much time here…man tends to forget how fine she is."

"Keep it that way."

"Well, sure *I* will." Barker rested a hand over his heart. "All your boys will. Well…maybe not." He chuckled. "Seriously though, if she's about to become a part of our lovely community, you'd do well to let everybody know she's yours, especially since you're in love with her."

"You're as backward as Linus and Tigo."

"In most things, yes," Barker agreed with a chuckle. "But I gotta agree with them in this case."

Eli pushed at one side of his shirt and smoothed a hand across the Seventy-Sixers emblem on the T-shirt beneath it. "I didn't plan this. I don't know what I planned but it sure as hell wasn't this. I don't know if I'm coming or going with her and I don't really care as long as she's there."

"And even after all that, you still can't admit you love her," Barker teased as a curious light came to his perfectly spaced gaze. "Or is that because you haven't told *her* yet? *Or* is he terrified?"

"He's terrified," Elias admitted, rolling his eyes when Barker laughed.

"Sorry, man, but it ain't every day one of the cool and collected loses a few points." Barker took a swig of the beer he'd ordered. "Word to the wise? Tell her how you feel. Chances are she feels the same and she's waitin' on *you* to say it first." He shrugged. "Women do that 'cause they're smart enough to know we run like hell when they say it first."

Eli broke into a laugh that had the women at a nearby table smiling in approval. "I can't wait to throw all this advice back at you when *that* woman walks into your life."

"Chances are I'll be too stupid to realize it's her, but thanks for the warning." Barker tilted back more beer. "Your memory ain't the best so chances are even higher that you'll forget it."

Head bowed, and attention focused on what she believed to be a very revealing notebook, Detective Sophia Hail walked the familiar corridor leading to her precinct office. As she spent most of her waking hours at the place, she knew it like the back of her hand and could maneuver the halls with her eyes closed.

With that in mind, the added fixture she found in her office set her completely off-kilter. It was a *fixture* that made the dimmed, cramped space of her office seem virtually matchbox size.

Santigo waited along the edge of her cluttered desk and watched Sophie linger in the doorway frowning over whatever held her interest.

"Soph?" His voice was as soft as the light in his probing eyes when he studied the surprise on her lovely milk-chocolate-colored face.

"Tigo…" she whispered, stepping inside the room as though she were being tugged by some invisible cord. Her bow-shaped mouth parted but no sound emerged.

"Hope you don't mind this?" Tigo knew she wouldn't. Sophia Hail was polite to a fault. A trait that she'd managed to hold on to despite the fact that her job rarely called for it.

"No, it's okay, um…" She smoothed a suddenly sweaty palm across the seat of her navy blue trousers. "It's been a long time."

"Not so long…" Tigo glanced at his hands rubbing one inside the other. "I saw you having lunch with Clarissa David remember?"

"Right." Sophie cleared her throat then and forced a touch more firmness into her voice. "What are you doing here, T?"

"Hoping no one's asked you to the Reed House Jazz Supper because I want to take you."

Sophie's expression proved the invite was the last thing she expected. "Um…I really, uh—" *Dammit, stop blinking!* she ordered herself. "I really haven't thought about it much."

"That's weird considering your parents started the place."

"Well, I've been busy."

"Does that mean you don't have a date?"

"I just said I've been busy."

"So you'll go with me."

"T—"

"I'll call you and we can talk details." He pushed off the desk.

Sophie's gray eyes were focused instantly on the awesome breadth of his shoulders. When he squeezed her elbow, she wanted to close her eyes and savor the sensation it rushed to her stomach.

"Good to see you," he spoke near her temple and tugged one of the spiral curls falling from her chignon.

Dazed, Sophie didn't register the knock to the door-jamb that came some two minutes after Tigo's departure. Finding the Chief of Detectives in her doorway caught her completely off guard.

"Sorry, sir." She straightened another inch.

"No worries." Paul Hertz was a tall thin man who never let his build stop him from throwing himself into the fray. He'd been known to be the first into a conflict and maintaining an active presence until the culprit was apprehended and his men were out of harm's way.

"You've been pretty preoccupied lately," Paul noted.

"A lot going on, sir."

"New case?" Paul scratched at the silvering hair along his sideburns.

"Not officially—" she sighed "—but if what I suspect is true, it could be one hell of a storm."

"Anything to report?"

Sophie appeared wary. "I want to be sure here, sir, before I say too much."

Paul was already nodding. "Understood. So was that Santigo Rodriguez I saw a few minutes ago?"

"Yeah…" Sophie's voice went soft again.

"Been a long time," Paul mentioned.

"Yeah." Sophie bowed her head briefly before looking up toward the bull pen. "It's been a very long time."

The sorely missed sounds of laughter filled Jaz Beaumont's home that evening. Clarissa decided that it'd be best to share her proposed plans with the dancers before they sat down to enjoy a meal. Her anxieties over the reactions to the announcement were unfounded. The girls were more excited than Clarissa had ever seen them, which was saying quite a lot.

The women also shared their own insights on Jaz

who had often spoken of Jaz's hopes for turning the club into a school where they could serve as instructors. They told Clarissa that they were sure those plans had died when Jaz did.

Following a delicious meal of robustly seasoned grilled turkey, rice, vegetables and buttered rolls, the group adjourned to the TV room for coffee and apple crumb cake.

"What's the timeline for the project?" Fredrika Tannen asked once everyone was settled with their first slice of cake.

"Well, I've continued the meetings Aunt Jaz was having with Joss Construction and I'll be meeting soon with the architects to discuss the changes. I hope to have more to tell you guys soon." She sighed and looked toward Rayelle.

"I want you all to know that I don't expect everyone to be excited by this. I'm proposing a school here. It'll be an opportunity for you all to teach *and* learn. You'll be salaried—any tips acquired may not be what you're used to." Clarissa tucked her legs beneath her on a white-and-gold-plaid Chippendale chair.

"This will be a slow transition, guys. The status quo will be in effect for another few years at least and then that part of the club may be slowly phased out. I promise each of you that no one will be left without a job if they want one."

Applause filled the room at such a volume that the doorbell could barely be heard above it. Ray left to answer it while Clarissa fielded questions regarding the operation of the school. The group launched a conversation about the teachers Clarissa had already been in touch with.

"How will these *learned instructors* treat us, Clarissa?" Morgan Beech asked, her tone skeptical.

"Yeah…" Sia Leonard agreed with the question. "Miss J never made us feel ashamed of our dancing, Clarissa."

"And neither will anyone else." Clarissa gave each woman the benefit of her gaze. "If it helps to know, the possible instructors I've spoken with are eager to work with experienced dancers whose backgrounds are…*diverse* from their own."

Laughter rose but the volume unfortunately could not muffle the sound of a loud voice—a loud, *angry* voice.

Silence gradually took its place as the women turned toward the room entrance. Soon, Rayelle had returned with a tight-lipped Waymon Cole in tow. The man wasted no time with greetings.

"I need to speak with you."

Nonplussed by the hard look directed her way, Clarissa stood. "There's plenty of cake, ladies. I don't want a slice left." She nodded stiffly when Waymon waved for her to precede him.

"Why wasn't I invited to your little party?" Waymon asked when they'd barely cleared the room.

"Is there a problem with me having a meeting with the dancers? Last time I looked, you weren't one."

"May I inquire about the topic of discussion?"

The warmth in Clarissa's brown eyes was replaced by a distinctly chillier one when she turned to him. "Something tells me it won't be a surprise to you."

"What's that supposed to mean?" His voice rose another angry decibel.

Clarissa folded her arms across the front of the coral and green asymmetrical T-shirt she sported. She kept her calm, though her temper was definitely beginning a slow simmer in response to the man loud-talking her in her own home.

"Jaz already mentioned it to the girls. She wanted to make it a reality."

Waymon shifted his stance. "What's this all about, Clarissa?"

"I'm planning to phase out the gentlemen's club for a dance studio."

The man's light caramel-toned complexion seemed closer to burgundy as his face flushed crimson. "Tell me you're not serious," he breathed.

"Very. It's what Aunt Jaz wanted."

"She also wanted to make money and I'm pretty sure those girls aren't ready to forfeit their dancers' pay to become teachers!"

"We've discussed that and that's *all* we're doing is *discussing*. Nothing's set in stone yet. I wanted to talk to the girls first."

"And what about the decision makers?" Waymon challenged.

"That would be me." Clarissa propped her hands to her hips. "In case you forgot, Jaz left the club to *me*."

"Humph." Waymon regarded Clarissa with something akin to respect but more closely resembling irritation. "You've certainly gotten into the swing of things sitting in the top chair."

"Feeling more and more comfy every day."

Waymon rolled his eyes toward the TV room entrance. "So is this *discussing* on the verge of turning into planning?"

"Could be."

"Need I remind you that I'm the club's business manager, so such things should be run by *me* first."

Clarissa smiled. "You were my *aunt's* business manager. But rest assured you'll be among the first to know when a decision's been made."

Waymon nodded abruptly as though taking note that the lines had been drawn. "You'd do well to remember that your aunt didn't run her club single-handedly," he said. "A lot of people have a stake in what goes on here."

"Good night, Waymon."

He fixed her with a pointed look and then left the house far more quietly than he'd arrived.

Chapter 14

Clarissa had her agenda planned in full for the next day. The unexpected visit from Waymon Cole the night before was as surprising as it was telling. Surprising in that Clarissa and Waymon had never had a cross word between them. He was her aunt's oldest friend, for heaven's sake!

It was, however, a telling conversation combined with all the strange pieces of information she had uncovered in the wake of her aunt's death. The suspicions Waymon now roused were too disturbing to be ignored.

Clarissa's first stop was to Dr. Steve Raines's practice. She could only hope he'd have time to see her. Following Waymon's visit, she contacted the doctor or rather his answering service to request a few moments of his time that morning. She had not received a call back to confirm the meeting.

* * *

A smiling middle-aged woman with waves of pecan-brown hair and sparkling green eyes greeted Clarissa when she arrived at Dr. Raines's office.

"Ms. David?" The woman spoke before Clarissa could say a word. "Miranda Sims. I knew your aunt. I was so very sorry to hear of her passing," the woman said once she'd rounded her desk.

"Thank you, Ms. Sims." Clarissa shook the woman's outstretched hand. "I apologize for just dropping by. I really do need to speak with the doctor. I don't mind waiting for whatever time he can spare."

"That won't be necessary, hon." Miranda smoothed a hand up and down the teal silk of Clarissa's blouse. "He's been expecting you. You're welcome to go right on in." Miranda waved toward an oak door in the distance.

Clarissa squeezed her hand again. "Thank you so much."

Steve Raines was making his way to the door when he called for Clarissa to enter. They welcomed one another with hugs. Steve kissed Clarissa's forehead and then led her to the beige suede living area in the office.

"How are you, love?" Steve Raines's lilting Kingston accent commanded relaxation. He leaned close and propped Clarissa's chin on his index finger. "You look tired."

"I've been working to make some changes at the club." She massaged her neck and smiled wearily. "Things Aunt Jaz wanted to do but never had the time for."

Steve patted Clarissa's knee in a fatherly manner. "What's wrong, love?"

"I guess I can't stop wondering if it was my aunt's health that led to her death. I just can't make myself believe that it was *that* bad." Clarissa rested her elbows to her knees. "There was so much she had planned for it all to be just taken away."

"I know it seems unfair." Steve moved closer to Clarissa on the sofa. "You should take comfort in knowing that Jazmina lived her life to the fullest." Steve's eyes twinkled with a sly merriment. "There was always one more thing that needed doing as far as she was concerned. She always wanted to have a plan. Said that when her time was up, it was just up. But she'd never just sit around and *wait* on it."

The doctor's words dried Clarissa sudden tears and replaced them with some contentment. "Did she take care of herself?" she asked.

Steve sighed. "Obviously not as well as she should have. Many times 'living life to the fullest' acts at cross purposes with taking care of one's health. But she knew exactly what she was doing. She was at peace and happy when she died. That had a lot to do with you, Clarissa." Steve blinked and focused on his hands for a weighty moment. "I found nothing that tells me she took her own life."

Clarissa inhaled deeply. She knew Jaz would never have done a thing like taking her own life. Steve, however, had provided a close-enough answer to the question she really wanted to as—which was whether anyone else had taken it.

Elias treasured the hug from his mother. He kept hold of her, taking comfort in the familiar yet missed scent of her perfume. When he kissed her cheek and pulled away, Lilia Joss kept her son close.

"Are you feeling all right, sweetness?" She felt his cheek, using the back of her hand.

"You're funny." Eli grinned, taking her hand and planting a kiss to her palm. Linking arms, they strolled from the foyer and into the living room.

"I know something's up." Lilia looked over to peer wisely into her son's handsome face. "You're coming to give me a rough time about letting Stan Crothers take me to the dinner at Reed House."

"I'm cool with you going with the man." Eli sighed as if it exhausted him to do so. "And I won't break Stan's heart by makin' trouble."

Lilia fixed Elias with a smug, playful look then. "So is this visit about *my* social life or yours…?"

Eli worked the bridge of his nose between his thumb and forefinger. "What have you heard?" he asked as though he had already imagined.

"Well, I really don't know much." Lilia perched her statuesque form on the back of the floral sofa and watched Eli walk on into the expansive room.

"You know her name."

"I do and I'd like to know why you tried to downplay it when I met Clarissa at the funeral?"

Eli bowed his head and shrugged. "I didn't know it'd become what it has."

Lilia released a happy gasp. "The guys said it was probably that serious."

Eli shook his head. "Linus and Tigo."

Lilia held her hands clasped against the strand of

pearls clinging to her shirt lapels. "So are you here to make an announcement?"

"I'm here because I think I love her—because I *know* I love her. I, um…I'm getting possessive."

"I see…" Lilia pressed her lips together and studied the sofa's pattern. She knew very well how seriously her son viewed things he'd become possessive over. Until now, those things had never included a woman.

Eli went to the sofa and took his mother by the hands. "How would you feel about that, Ma?" He kept his eyes on her hands. "Clarissa being who she is and all."

Lilia's wide, lovely eyes glowed teasingly. "Who is she?"

Eli wasn't amused. "Don't, Ma—not after what her aunt did. Not to mention that Clarissa's a dead ringer for the woman."

"Eli." Lilia shook her head. "I could never hate that girl or judge her for that. She's a child and she's *not* her aunt."

"She's only a reminder."

"Yet *you* managed to fall in love with her."

Eli scratched the curling hair tapered at his neck. "I don't want to hurt you, Mama."

Lilia crossed her arms over her chest. "So you're saying you'd give her up for me?

"Raising you wasn't easy, Elias," Lilia went on when Eli offered no reply to her question. "Considering the fact that I did most of the raising myself. So please don't make me believe I raised an idiot."

"Mama—"

"Hush." She waved a hand for emphasis. "Now this

is really *none* of your business but circumstances are obviously calling for clarification." She left the sofa.

Eli claimed the place his mother vacated. Silent, he watched her walk the perimeter of the bright room.

"Your father was a tramp." She bit out the words but managed to add a short laugh. "I guess he got it honest given that his daddy couldn't keep his pants up to save his life." Her laughter came through more genuine then. "They were a couple of real characters—must've been somethin' in those blue eyes."

"Right…" Eli grimaced. "I know.…"

Lilia turned. "But what you *don't* know is Jaz Beaumont wasn't the only woman or even the most dramatic one for that matter. She's just the one you were old enough to remember." Lilia eased her hands into her cream-colored pinstriped trousers and studied her garden from the living room window.

"I think Jaz was the last one and I owe that to the late Ms. Beaumont herself."

"Mama, what are you talking about?" Eli's deep voice was a whisper.

"It was Jaz Beaumont who talked your father out of leaving us." She smiled wanly. "It was no secret that Jaz had known plenty of other women's husbands and she regretted that, but she'd never taken a father away from his kids and she wasn't about to start." Lilia turned away from the garden to look at Eli.

"She told Evan that he had a woman—a lady—a *real* lady… She told him I'd given him a beautiful son whom she could look at and tell was going to make him proud and be a beacon for his business. She told him that was something she'd never have."

"How do you know all this?" Eli was riveted by the story.

"She told us together." Lilia made her way back across the room. "Your father broke down crying right there in the office at that club of hers. Apologized to me 'til he was hoarse and said he was sorry for everything. Squeezed my hands so tight, I thought he'd break 'em." Lilia flexed her hands and smiled down at them.

"There's never any way to be one hundred percent about anything, but I don't think he ever stepped out again. If he did, he showed me so much love and attention that I never had cause to ever suspect him afterward." She returned to sit next to Eli along the back of the sofa.

"I know Evan's one regret was that he'd damaged you." She brushed her fingers down Eli's cheek.

"I know all you remember of your father is how unhappy he made me and that did a lot to shape the man you are now."

"I don't want to hurt Clarissa that way." His jaw clenched and he shook his head. "She's too good for that."

"Baby, *all* women are too good for that, yet some men seem to think there are those of us who enjoy shabby treatment. Some women accept it, having had so many dismal encounters that they start to believe they aren't worthy of more."

Lilia gave Eli's knee a hard pat. "If you're serious about Clarissa, then prove it. Be honest with her and treat her like you remember every day that she's 'too good' for anything less."

Eli pulled his mother close and murmured the words "thank you" next to her cheek.

Clarissa followed her visit with Steve Raines with one to Jaz's attorney, Martin Rath. Clarissa was shown into Martin's stark office without having to wait. The man received her with hugs and a humorous greeting that had her laughing and at once at ease.

"And how are you?" Martin cupped both hands about Clarissa's face to scrutinize her. "Not working too hard, are we? Don't answer that, of course you are. You're Jaz's niece, after all." Placing his hand at the small of her back, Martin escorted Clarissa to one of the deep square chairs before his black desk.

"It's good that you stopped in. We're all set to have a powwow over the estate planning or if that's too involved, we can arrange a simple overview about the extent of Jaz's holdings."

"Thanks, Martin." Clarissa patted the man's hand to get him to calm down. "Any of that sounds fine for a later time. I, uh…I'm sorry for just stopping by like this. Just couldn't wait."

Out of habit, Martin pushed at the grayish-blond hair that frequently fell into his eyes. The bluish orbs reflected concern.

"What's this about, dear?"

"Martin, did my aunt have any business concerns?"

"Concerns? You mean with the club?"

"I mean did she have any reason to think there was something underhanded going on?"

"Underhanded as in…?"

"Anything." Clarissa had always liked and respected

Martin. After her conversation with Waymon though, she didn't know who to trust.

"If she did, she never said anything to me." Martin rubbed his jaw. "Nothing specific anyway."

Clarissa fingered a clipped lock of her hair. "What does that mean?"

"There was the day she came to change her will."

Clarissa blinked. "So she hadn't planned to leave me everything?"

"Oh, no. No, dear. All Jaz owned was yours and that was the way she wanted it. All but the club. She had that set for different hands."

"Why?" Her brown eyes reflected hurt.

"Jaz didn't want you tied to the place your whole life the way she'd been." Martin leaned over to rest his elbows on his knees. "Not that she didn't love the business but she thought you could have more—a beautiful life, children, a man to love and take care of you—all the things she'd wanted for herself.

"When she came to change the will, she told me she'd worked too hard to make her business a long-standing and lucrative establishment to let it be turned into something filthy and corrupt. She said she'd known filthy and corrupt too well to ever go back to it."

"Martin? Can you tell me who she had in mind to take the club?"

Again, Martin patted Clarissa's hand. "It was Waymon Cole."

"Oh." Clarissa's disappointment was difficult to miss.

Elias shut down the Navigator's ignition. "Oh?" he prompted.

"I just thought…" She bit her lip while looking past the passenger window toward the restaurant entrance. "I thought we were staying in for dinner."

"I see." He leaned over the gear shift to retrieve his wallet from the glove compartment. "Don't you think we've stayed in enough?"

"Is this about business?"

"Why would you think that?"

"Well, I—" Clarissa blinked and glanced toward the restaurant entrance again. "It's just that no one knows we're…"

Smiling, Elias placed his wallet in an inside pocket of the champagne-colored suit coat he wore. He gave her his full attention then. "You were saying?"

Clarissa felt her cheeks burn.

"No one knows we're…what, Clari?"

Boldly, she faced him across the gear shift. "Are you ready for people to know we're sleeping together?"

Elias laughed and loudly. "I promise I won't shout it out in the dining room!" He kissed her hard and then left the SUV.

Clarissa eyed him suspiciously as he helped her from the step rail making sure the black chiffon draping over the pants of her jumpsuit didn't catch in the chic Vera Wang pumps she sported.

"What's this all about?" she asked.

He shut the passenger door but wouldn't let her move any farther. "This is about me taking my girl out for dinner." He offered her his arm.

Clarissa accepted and received a kiss for her trouble.

At the entrance, the maître d' recognized them

both. The man addressed Clarissa fondly and kissed her cheek.

"How is it I never met you before that day in Crothers's shop?" Eli queried as they followed the host through the dining room.

"I don't know." She shrugged and looked up to grace him with a wink. "Maybe it was time for your luck to change."

Eli dipped his head closer. "Damn right," he agreed, seconds before plying Clarissa with another kiss while they waited.

Of course every eye followed the heated exchange. Whispers soon ran rampant regarding the unexpected couple. When Elias broke their kiss, Clarissa was riveted on what she saw in his uncommon eyes.

"What is going on with you?"

Elias only grinned at her question.

"Well, this is right out in the open," Clarissa noted once they were seated at the table.

Eli kept his eyes on the menu he held. "If I didn't know better, I'd swear you're ashamed to be seen with me."

Clarissa pulled a few pink petals from their floral centerpiece and tossed them in his direction.

"What?" Eli brushed the pieces from his lap. "How am I to know? Maybe I'm not your sort of guy. Being from California and all… How do I know you're not more interested in those surfer types?"

Clarissa's laughter took hold softly but consistently until they were interrupted.

"Eli!"

"Robb!" Elias stood to shake hands with the grinning

prematurely gray gentleman who had turned a probing eye on Clarissa.

"I don't believe I've had the pleasure."

Elias drew the man closer to the table. "Robert Tipman, Clarissa David. Clarissa's in town seeing to final business for her aunt Jaz Beaumont."

"Ah, yes." Robb's expression grew more subdued. "I'm sorry for your loss, Ms. David."

Robb was still holding Clarissa's hand when his date approached. The full-figured brunette was clearly none too pleased by what she saw.

"Baby, this is Clarissa David, Eli's girl," Robb explained before the woman could say anything untoward. "Clarissa, this is Melanie Shales."

"Ms. Shales." Clarissa shook hands with the flabbergasted woman who regarded her with a mix of awe and surprise.

"Yikes," Clarissa noted when the couple had strolled off. "One would think you never take out a date."

"It's not that." Eli was back to studying his menu. "I just never brought anyone else here to eat except for my mother." He looked her way then.

Clarissa blinked owlishly, taking note of the unreadable glint in his blue-green stare.

"Well, that's sweet." She reached for a water glass and helped herself to a long swallow. "Sweet that you have a special place for you and your mom."

Elias caught her hand when she would have reached for the glass again. He kissed the back of it and studied the spot his mouth had brushed. "It's a special place for the women that I love."

Clarissa felt her lips part. Her hand went weak inside his. "Eli."

He studied her reaction. "Does that scare you?"

"Does *what* scare me?"

Elias smiled, understanding that she expected him to be more specific with his confession.

"I love you, Clarissa David."

"Because—"

"Because you let me be your first?" He shrugged and relaxed in his chair. "Maybe. Because you've got me so turned around that I don't know whether I'm coming or whether I'm going? Maybe definitely. Because you put your own life on hold to give your aunt happiness and peace of mind? That, too." His gaze narrowed and he raked her collarbone and the almond-brown swells of her breasts above the banded strapless bodice of her jumpsuit.

"And on top of all that, an incredible body and face which I'm not too proud to admit snagged me from the jump, how could a package this provocative inside and out not command a man's attention and emotion?"

"What is it?" She managed to question the sudden cloud that filtered his fantastic caramel-doused features.

"Remember what I said to you about tying yourself to a man like me? The stock I come from and how the men in my family have treated the women they supposedly love?" He rubbed his thumb into the center of his palm. "I don't know whether I'll ever stop being terrified by the possibility that I could ever do that to you, but that doesn't terrify me half as much as letting you walk away without telling you how I feel and working like hell to keep you with me." He swallowed hard and looked a smidge uncertain. "That is, if you—if you feel the same…"

"I love you, Elias Joss. Because you were my first? Maybe. Because you unfairly label yourself as untrustworthy and something about that breaks my heart and makes me want to prove to you how wrong that is? Perhaps. Because you're exceptionally gorgeous and I love looking into your eyes? Mmm…very definitely. How could a package this—provocative inside and out—not command a woman's attention and emotion?"

Uncertainty vanishing, Elias left his chair and moved to Clarissa's side of the table. There, he knelt before her, treating her to a kiss that sent conversation spiraling in the crowded dining room.

Chapter 15

It took Elias some time to unlock his front door, what with holding Clarissa in his arms and kissing her senseless. Once inside, he kept her pressed against the front door for some time. Clarissa clung to him, deepening the kiss as Eli's touch grew bolder. She let him have his way, fondling her outside and inside her clothes before he removed them and carried her through the foyer. He charted a direct path for his bedroom.

Clarissa was clothed only in her bra and panties by the time Elias deposited her on his bed. There, he proceeded to drive her out of her mind with the gliding and suckling of his lips and tongue.

Unexpectedly, Clarissa turned the tables when Eli set out to remove her underthings. She straddled his lap, pulling him out of the champagne-colored suit coat and unbuttoning the cream shirt that complemented his complexion. Her nails raked his sleek chest before she replaced them with her mouth to treat his nipples to the same suckling he had subjected her to.

Elias curved his fingertips into her short glossy hair, relishing the attention she gave him. Clarissa made quick work of his belt and trouser fastening. She focused her attention below his waist for several moments.

"Clari…wait…"

"Shh…" She gave him no respite and pleasured him with a tender enthusiasm that threatened to stifle his breathing.

When she ended the sensual assault and moved up to instigate a different kind of kiss, Eli clutched her hips. He guided them in subtle rotations against his erect shaft. As Clarissa was still garbed in the lacy pair of white panties, the barrier of material against his sensitive flesh threw his hormones into a frenzy.

Clarissa ended their kiss, rising above Eli that time to undo the back clasp of the bra covering her breasts. She let the garment drop as he brought his hands up to squeeze and weigh the mounds until her nipples were puckered from his attentions. When his hands lowered again, one cupped her hip while the other curved over her thigh and this thumb went to work on her clit.

His extraordinary stare followed the flutter of her lashes and tilt of her head as he stimulated her. She circled and ground against him yet she tried to hold at bay the orgasm which was fast approaching. Clarissa had hoped to be in more control of the act that night. As usual, Eli's touch commanded her reaction.

"How long will you make me wait, Clari?" he asked after grunting a curse of impatience.

"How long are you *willing* to wait?" She felt a bit more in control then until she found herself jerked into another kiss. In the midst of it, Elias rummaged in the nightstand drawer for a condom.

Clarissa slapped at his hand and took charge of the search until she found one of the square foil packets. Again, she tortured him with a few additional hip rotations that had Eli taking her derriere in his palms and commanding her moves with a definite force. She shuddered on the sensation of the orgasmic waves of pleasure that filled her. Wearily, she took hold of a sliver of control and ceased her hip moves midrotation.

"Damn you," Eli almost growled.

Clarissa merely smiled while applying the condom, slowly. She handled the task as though it were a caress and Eli worked the heels of his hands into his eyes as he groaned.

Clarissa finished setting the condom in place, and then she settled herself in one fluid move. Eli thrust upward the moment she was fully enveloping his sex in hers. One hand held on to her hip while the other pressed against her belly.

Elias worked his thumb into her navel to feel the alluring stabs of arrogance mixed with possession as he studied the changes in her expression. He could tell that she was completely overcome by the things he did to her.

Clarissa had no intention of being the only one overcome by desire. She switched the direction of her hips over him. Suddenly weakened, Eli's hands drifted from her body to rest upon the rumpled covers. All energy flowed to his hips then and together the lovers merged into a heated, energetic rhythm. The sounds of their moans were evoked by their compatibility and the love that fueled it.

Later, Clarissa and Eli lounged in bed. The room was lit only by a thin beam of moonlight.

"I was about fifteen or so when I realized how much my virginity meant to my aunt." She smiled and bumped her chin on the hand resting on Eli's abdomen. "At first I didn't get what the big deal was and then my dad sent me to stay with her that summer."

Eli rested with one arm across his eyes, his free hand played in the tousle of Clarissa's hair. He massaged her neck a bit more intently when she grew quiet. He knew that memories of her aunt had to still feel quite raw in the wake of the woman's death.

"I got the full education on exactly what she did for a living," Clarissa was saying. "I understood what kind of woman people saw her as…knew her to be." She laid her cheek flat on his abs then.

"But she was a woman who truly had a golden heart. The way she cared for those girls…and they really needed someone to care." She smirked and thought over her words. "The way some of them lived, the horrors they'd been through. I guess I got caught up in what drove my aunt."

"And you wanted to save them, too," Eli guessed, caressing the shell of her ear and a curl that clung to it.

"Not if you mean by getting them out of dancing." She shook her head awkwardly against him. "I just wanted to be sure they knew there were more opportunities available to them and ways that didn't involve men taking pleasure for money of all things."

"So you made that your own mission and forgot to live."

"I've lived." She raised her head and shrugged. "But I admit I may have been influenced by the problems those girls had. Guess I was determined not to let myself be put in heartbreaking positions because of men."

Eli whistled. "You know I've heard that can be an unfortunate side effect of love."

Clarissa smiled and snuggled in next to him. "I realized that—eventually. At first keeping my virginity was about my aunt's expectations and then it was about not wanting to be like the girls and then…" She let the word evaporate into a sigh. "Then I realized all that was a crock. All of it came down to me—just me lying to myself. I was just too…nervous to…I don't know, to take a chance. I was too afraid of that possible heartbreak."

Elias gathered her close. "Does it help to know that I'm nervous and afraid, too?"

Clarissa looked up but could see nothing—not even the ethereal blue of his eyes. She didn't need that consolation. His voice was assurance enough. She inched up to find his mouth.

"It helps," she spoke against his lips. "It helps more than you know."

Clarissa could have had her pick of escorts that day, all of them courtesy of Philadelphia's finest. Male detectives working the desk when she appeared were all too happy to volunteer to show their lovely visitor into Sophie Hail's office.

"Thanks, guys." Sophie greeted her coworkers with a double wave and smile in response to their unnecessary and clearly self-serving gesture. She waited until they took their leave before turning to her visitor.

"Hey, Clarissa. Sorry about that." She waved to a chair before her desk.

"They're sweet," Clarissa excused.

"Guess so." Sophie scrunched her nose in reply. "Long as a woman knows and stays in her place."

"Which is off the force." Clarissa settled into a worn leather chair. "I suppose a woman has to be dedicated to do a job like this—it takes its toll."

"Yeah…" Sophie's expression turned thoughtful. "It takes a toll on a lot of things." She then tapped her nails to the desk and offered up a resolute smile. "I guess you're here to discuss what I found in Jazmina's notebook?"

"I can guess well enough." Clarissa recrossed her jean-clad legs. "Rayelle and me…we knew it was probably a long shot that you'd find anything." She braced her elbows on the thin metal arms of the chair. "These notes were just so weird—cryptic—and then after I talked to you…" She threw her head back and grinned.

"They were dress sizes for the girl's costumes, right?" Clarissa offered.

"I wouldn't be so quick to say that." Sophie twirled a curl of hair around her index finger and reclined in her seat. "One could take this easily for a ledger."

"A ledger?" Clarissa scooted up in her seat. "For what?"

"Well, that's the question." Sophie massaged her eyes. "If only I had had the chance to talk with your aunt one last time. I may've at least gotten a name." She looked down at the supposed "ledger" lying flat open on the desk.

"All these strange numbers…one column in particular—strange in a way I can't put a finger on," she said even while running a finger down the page.

"Did my aunt ever give you a hint about anybody?" Sophie only shook her head.

Clarissa licked her lips and leaned forward. "Not even Waymon Cole?"

Sophie shook her head but included a frown that time. "Why does that name sound so familiar?"

"He's one of my aunt's oldest friends and her business manager, as well."

"Aah…" Sophie's frown was replaced by curiosity. She swiveled her chair to and fro tugging at the cuff of her olive-green blouse. "You think this Mr. Cole could have something to do with what's in this book?"

"I never would have thought that before a very strange conversation I had with the man." Clarissa spent the next twelve minutes discussing Waymon's adversity to the changes she was proposing for the club.

"You know that could be nothing more than the man showing concern over his friend's business."

Clarissa propped her fist to her chin. "I hope that's all it is."

"Boys!" Cleveland Echols greeted Elias and Barker with hugs and handshakes when he found them in his office that afternoon. Echols was a rotund man of average height whose gregarious nature was rivaled only by his generous heart.

"What are you drinking?" Cleveland Echols asked once the younger men had assured him that their mothers were doing just fine.

"Got a fine new Scotch over here," Cleve announced.

Elias and Barker exchanged looks while the man worked at the bar.

"You're a hard man to get in touch with Mr. Cleve," Eli said. "I haven't been able to reach you since we talked about our now nonexistent project."

"Yes…" Cleve passed drinks to the men. "And I am sorry that we had to cancel out on that."

Barker jumped on the opening. "Eli said the cancellation had to do with a loss of your investors to Waymon Cole."

Cleve provided a stiff nod and sipped on his drink.

"Did they have problems being tied to a man whose customers include suspected drug dealers?"

"There are all kinds of criminals in the world, Barker," Cleve snapped and went to sit behind his desk. "The worst are the ones who come dressed in the most legitimate apparel."

"Sir, we know the investors are cops' wives." Eli saw the change in Cleveland's expression. "We know they live all over the country."

Cleve leaned forward to set his glass to the desk and almost missed the edge. "How do you…know that?"

"Sir, we really don't know a thing—especially why these people dropped out of the bank project *or* why they set out to ruin your business and your other projects." Eli dipped his head a fraction. "Unless you're about to tell us that they hadn't done that."

Cleveland finished his drink. "You guys don't want to know this."

"I'm sure we do, sir," Barker confirmed.

Cleve laughed. "You think you'll get a story out of it, boy? Broadcast a big report? They'd never allow it."

"Because cops are involved," Eli guessed.

Cleveland shook his head. "These aren't just a group of corrupt uniforms walkin' a beat. These are seasoned public servants with rank and pull—they've got the ability to make the lives of their enemies a living hell."

Eli leaned back in his chair, looking as if he'd found an answer to at least one of his questions. "So it *is* the cops and not their wives."

Cleve went back to the bar for another drink. "The wives were a front, I'm not even sure half of 'em know their husbands had used their names."

"What's goin' on, Mr. Cleve?" Barker leaned forward in his chair.

Cleve threw back the second drink with barely a wince. "It's about money, what else?" He bowed his head for a lengthy moment and then faced Elias and Barker.

"I don't know who had the genius idea to put this all in motion, but this is about money. Drug money—a lot of it. It's about finding a way to secure it."

"Money laundering," Elias noted.

Cleve studied the glass emptied of liquor and smirked. "A few cops out West had funneled money through a club, used the girls, tipped big, booked private parties, weekend performances…" He set the glass to the bar with unnecessary force.

"It went great 'til the club owner got greedy and demanded a bigger cut. The guys who came up with what we've got going here still thought the idea was sound. They figured they just needed to tweak the implementation to make it work better."

Cleveland fixed a wan smile to his thick lips. "Some of my alleged drug dealing customers already had accounts here as did a few of Philly's finest. It was a nice marriage." He shrugged. "But then the money kept growing and transporting it became an issue."

Eli grinned ill-humoredly. "I guess that cops coming into the bank with bags of money could raise suspicions."

"So they brought Waymon Cole in on the deal. Jazzy B's was perfect for what they had in mind." Cleveland folded his arms over the front of his suit coat. "High-end strippers and there were some who didn't mind crossing the lines. The money tumbled in like a wave and it wasn't long before these newly wealthy cops figured they should have their *own* bank hence the project with Joss Construction. It could have been the perfect set-up."

"Only?" Eli asked.

"*Only* the owner got suspicious."

"Jaz Beaumont."

Cleve nodded toward Barker. "Somehow she found out that the bank had two accounts for the club. Cole wasn't expecting that. Jaz had never cared about the money—she always left that part to him."

Cleve walked back to his desk. "I talked to her myself—told her that I was sure it was a clerical error and that I'd check it out, but I knew that wouldn't pacify her for long. I got scared." He rubbed a hand across his mouth.

"The girl who was the courier for the club, she… We were… Cole knew about her—said *they'd* tell my wife if I breathed a word. But they set out to ruin my business anyway—shaking down my clients, ruining their business whether they were legitimate or not."

"Mr. Cleve—"

"Save it, Eli." Cleve threw up a hand.

"Sir, you could ruin 'em," Elias argued. "Throw 'em to the wolves—testify."

"At what price?" Cleve's warm gaze was suddenly full of venom. "I was fool enough to get caught up in this mess. I can't be responsible for having that girl's blood spilled. Jaz was good enough to hide her when she went to her complaining about some obsessive fan. I can't risk them finding her and doing her harm."

"It doesn't have to be that way, sir."

Cleve laughed over Eli's certainty. "And pray tell, son, why—after all that's happened—should it turn out any better?"

Chapter 16

That night Clarissa was on call for Jazzy B's. She had avoided the place—the floor and the customers, especially since Jazmina's death. Memories of happier times there were still too prevalent for her to feel completely at ease inside the establishment where she had cut her teeth en route to being a businesswoman.

Even so, she made her way through the club that night looking radiant and feeling rather jubilant. Their visit to Philly had carried her along the full spectrum of emotions, she believed. She had wallowed on the lowest levels of despair yet managed to taste the sweetness of a love that she had never expected.

Clarissa shook hands with a number of people—men and women alike. Jazzy B's Gentlemen's Club hadn't been exclusively for gentlemen in a long time. Women took in the shows as avidly as their male counterparts—

sometimes even more so. That night, the club's patrons held something else in common—mourning the loss of Jazmina Beaumont.

Clarissa received streams of condolences on her aunt's passing. It took close to an hour to cross from one side of the lower level to the other; there were just that many people. She had almost cleared the room, when a pair of arms encircled her waist and hands nudged the silver chain belt around the black split skirt that barely reached her midthigh.

"What are my chances on grabbing a private dance?" The man's voice was low against Clarissa's ear.

Her elbow was poised for the man's midsection but Clarissa hesitated. "A private dance…it'll cost you and I *am* seeing someone who might frown on that. Oh, what the hell? Meet me in the manager's office and we'll discuss it."

The man's arm went limp around Clarissa's waist, but he quickly recovered. Taking her by the elbow, he turned her to face him.

She dissolved into peals of laughter over the half-stunned, half-amused expression on his face.

Eli began to nod as if to concede that he had been thoroughly punked. With a resigned look softening his very seductive features, he sighed softly and then bent to tug her across his shoulder.

"That'll cost you," he grumbled. "Where's this office of yours?"

"I think you've got this backward, sugar. *You're* the one who's supposed to come out of pocket," Clarissa teased once they were locked inside the office.

"You're the only one coming out of anything." Eli's persuasive voice was a growl. He kept her against the door and attempted to kiss her out of the slinky, lacy, capped-sleeved blouse she wore.

"Not here, Eli," Clarissa sang.

"Oh—sorry. How about here?" Eli moved his hand up from her hip to cup a breast and squeeze.

"Someone might—" she shivered when he thumb started grazing the nipple that protruded against the sheer black fabric of her shirt "—someone might need me." She made a serious effort to resist him, though her defenses were surely weakening.

"Damn right someone might need you," he murmured. His mouth followed the path of his hand. His nose charted a trail between the fragrant valley of her bosom.

"Eli, please." She eventually pushed more strength into her voice. "Ray's off tonight and I need to be available." She started to tug the open collar of his gray shirt with increased persistence.

"It's gonna be pretty crazy here until all our new protocols are put in place."

Clearly reluctant to let her go, Elias pulled his face free of the perfumed cleavage but refused to release her from the trap between the door and his body.

"New protocols?" he queried, curiosity working its way into the vivid bluish-green of his stare. "What's Waymon Cole got to say about that?"

"Waymon?" Clarissa crossed her arms over her chest as almost laughed the man's name.

Eli shrugged, resting his shoulder against the door.

"Everyone knows he was your aunt's right hand around this place. I know he was very good at his job—still is."

"And how do you know that?" Clarissa followed suit and rested her shoulder on the door, as well.

"Man's gotta be pretty damn good at his job to be responsible for one of my deals falling through."

"Waymon." Clarissa spoke the name with a dash more reverence that time.

"A business deal with a man named Cleveland Echols." Eli focused on straightening the scalloped collar of Clarissa's blouse. "Cole got all his investors to walk out on his project—our project. Guess cops' wives are suckers for smooth talkers."

Clarissa gave a jerky shake of her head. "Cops' wives?" Clarissa moved from the door, considering the information as she walked the room's perimeter.

"Looks like your Mr. Cole is going into the bank-building business."

"Banks."

Eli grinned and settled back fully against the door. He pushed both hands into trouser pockets hidden by the hem of his shirt. "Why do I feel like I just gave you a piece to a puzzle?"

Clarissa eventually tuned in to the question. She blinked at Eli, dumbfounded at first and then with more awareness before she shook her head.

Eli pulled her close again, peering down into the dusky brown pools of her eyes with a look that was chilly in its intensity.

"Are you looking into suspicions about your aunt's clubs?"

"What?" She blinked more rapidly now. "Where'd you get that?"

"Am I right?"

Clarissa searched his striking blue orbs as if she were trying to uncover a truth, and then she grimaced. "She had some questions."

"About?"

"About why he bit my head off when he found out I was considering turning the club into a dance studio."

The confirmation turned Eli's eyes a darker tinge. He bit down so hard on his jaw that the muscle there twitched ominously.

"Is there any way that I could convince you to step back from this?" he asked.

"Eli?" She tilted her head at a curious angle. "What else do you know? And please spare me the protection thing—we don't have the time for it." She raised a hand to curb the confrontation welling in his stare.

"I have a friend on the police force who's helping me look into this," she said. "Elias, if you know something, I'd be really grateful if you'd share it."

Eli turned away, stroking his goatee as he walked the office. "This friend of yours, do you trust them?"

"Yes." She nodded with certainty. "So did Jaz. She was already sharing info about her suspicions with Sophie before she died."

"Sophie? Sophie...Hail?"

"Right—you—you know her?"

"She and Tigo had a thing. It was a long time ago."

Clarissa blinked to confirm what she already realized.

"Clari, will you step back from this?"

"Tell me what you know," she snapped.

He sat on the arm of a sofa. "I have a friend, too. One who's willing to break this thing wide open but he's protecting someone. A girl who used to work for your aunt. She hid her, believing that she was hiding the girl from some obsessed customer." He shrugged sleek brows in Clarissa's direction.

"Maybe Sophie can find her," he suggested. "My friend won't talk unless he knows this girl is safe."

"That's it." Discovery blossomed and Clarissa raised a hand to her cheek. "Cleve Echols, of course... Waymon, you son of a bitch."

"I expect you to stay away from the man, Clarissa." Elias kept his eyes on his palm where his thumb drove circles into the center. "Clarissa?"

"Yes. Yes, Eli." She gave the answer he wanted to hear.

His resulting smirk had nothing to do with amusement and little to do with confidence. "What time do I pick you up for the Humanitarian thing tomorrow?"

At first, Clarissa looked bewildered but then she remembered. "Seven," she said finally.

"I'll wait around out there until you're done here and take you home." He left the sofa then, fixing her with a lingering look before taking his leave.

When Elias was gone, Clarissa went to the phone and made a call to Detective Sophia Hail.

"Most of the people in this room couldn't stand my aunt," Clarissa remarked through clenched teeth. "They've got to hate it that she's being given this award now."

Eli worked his fingers along the rear row of shiny onyx buttons leading down from the choke collar of the lovely gray chiffon-over-satin gown that Clarissa wore. In spite of the slight touch, he could still feel her unease.

"From what I understand about the Breck process for considering its Humanitarian award recipients, no one is just *given* the award." He firmed his hold on her upper arms and made her face him. "She earned this, Clari."

Clarissa patted his hand, cupping her cheek. "That means a lot coming from you—considering all that she did."

Eli grunted and looked around the room of elegantly dressed guests. "It's funny how wrong a person can be about someone." His bright eyes followed the movement of his fingers rubbing her clipped dark hair. "How can I hate a woman who helped raise someone so incredible?"

The lovers were kissing when Leta Fields, chairperson for the committee, walked over to greet them and to bestow further congratulations.

"I'm only accepting the award, Leta. The real honor is my aunt's."

"Well said." Leta reached out to squeeze Clarissa's shoulder. "Let's get you two over to the table." She linked arms with both Clarissa and Elias.

At Jazmina Beaumont's table, several more well-wishers waited, including Waymon Cole.

"Humph, surprise, surprise." Clarissa sighed when she approached the wide round table with Leta and Elias.

Waymon appeared cool as always. "Not such a surprise I think. One of my dearest friends is being honored tonight for all of her work. I intend to be here for it."

He rubbed his palms together and regarded the group around the table. "I hope others will understand her sacrifice and how much her work—her club meant to her."

Subconsciously, Clarissa curled her fingers more tightly into Eli's jacket sleeve. "Well, we all know what Jaz's work meant to her. Her greatest hope for the club was for it to not fall into corruption." She waited for Waymon's eyes to meet hers. "I intend to make sure it doesn't."

"Everyone, I'd like for you to meet Elias Joss," she said before Waymon could respond to her challenge.

Whatever tension that may have been present at the table vanished shortly thereafter. Someone began to share a memory of Jazmina and laughter swirled around the table.

The Breck Humanitarian recipients were well received and well honored for their accomplishments. Those in attendance however were most interested in the acceptance of Jazmina Monike Beaumont's award, which was received by her niece.

Clarissa's speech was a testament to her love for her aunt as well as a pointed observation of those who had never allowed Jaz to forget what she was or accept that she had risen above it. Clarissa's speech ended on a high note however when she announced her plans for the proposed Beaumont Studio.

Not everyone was pleased with the powerful speech.

"May I speak with you?" Elias subtly intruded on Clarissa's conversation with a few of the Breck committee members. His hand was on her upper arm and he was already drawing her away from the crowd before she could politely excuse herself from the discussion.

"Eli, what—"

"What the hell are you doing?" he asked once they were sequestered in a corridor behind the banquet room.

"I thought I was trying to have a conversation."

"Don't play with me, Clari. I don't want you provoking Cole."

"I'm not afraid of him, Eli."

"Maybe you should be."

"Maybe I *would* be," Clarissa conceded with a shrug, "if I just weren't so damn mad over it."

Eli's face was unreadable then. "Anger is dangerous, Clari. Trust me, I know that."

"Yeah, I keep forgetting that." Cool accusation flooded Clarissa's expressive browns. "Maybe that's why you can't understand it. You hated my aunt like everybody else."

"You're being an idiot." He rolled his eyes.

"Why? Because I won't let you dictate to me?" she snapped as she observed him hotly. "Do you think you're entitled to that because you were my first?"

Elias waved a hand. "I can't talk to you."

"Then I guess you won't mind me walking away then?"

Eli was ready to follow of course, yet he steeled himself against engaging his baser instincts. Applying a hard massage to the base of his neck, he quietly ordered himself to let her go.

"This is quite a story, Detective."

Sophie Hail nodded. Her back was ramrod straight

as she sat before the desk. "I understand that, sir, but the evidence more than speaks for itself." She pressed on while making the case for her Captain Roy Poltice.

"Those strange numbers in the notebook from Jazmina Beaumont's office were badge numbers. They looked so familiar but I couldn't place them until I looked in the mirror one night. They're recorded backward in the book, sir.

"A few of those numbers are from the badges of members in our own squad, sir." She cleared her throat softly and looked down at her interlaced fingers.

"Chief of Detectives Paul Hertz was one of them, sir. His wife works for WPXI and she was one of Waymon Cole's investors."

"Christ..." Roy Poltice massaged his fingers into one of his bushy salt-and-pepper brows.

"The other column of numbers is the money each cop sent into the club and what I suspect is Waymon Cole's cut. Cleve Echols was cooperative enough to share some very revealing bank statements."

"And he's willing to testify to this?" Poltice asked.

Sophie nodded. "Now that he knows Rena Johnson is safe and willing to corroborate his story. It all connects, sir."

"Doesn't cause it to stink any less." Poltice groaned. "You know you're about to open up a can of worms the size of the Liberty Bell?"

"I know that, sir."

"Do you really?" Poltice leaned his broad form closer to his desk. "You're about to make a lot of enemies, Detective."

"Sir, a good woman and her niece trusted me enough

to bring me in on this. The least I can do is to see it through." She pursed her lips for a second. "I do hope I can count on you to help me do that, sir."

Poltice nodded. "You're a good cop, Hail, and since my butt is now on the line with yours, you damn well better make this thing stick."

"Sir," Sophie acknowledged the charge.

"So how do you want to handle this?" Poltice asked.

Sophie allowed her superior to see her smug smile. "Very publicly, sir."

One Week Later...

The Reed House Jazz Supper wasn't the average pot-luck dinner. Plates started at a cool one thousand dollars and went up to ten thousand. The benefits of such lavishness spoke volumes. Clarissa arrived alone but she didn't remain that way for long. She accepted countless congrats on the Humanitarian award that her aunt had received posthumously. Leta Fields arrived to give her last-minute tips on the presentation of the check to Reed House from the Breck committee.

Clarissa was waiting on a drink at the bar when she was turned around and pulled into the most thorough kiss. Melting, she entwined her tongue around Eli's, boldly arching herself into his devastatingly tuxedoed frame.

"Forgive me?" he asked after pulling back from their kiss.

She smiled. "For caring? There's nothing to forgive for that."

His sky-blue stare narrowed playfully. "So why'd you give me such a hard time about it then?"

Clarissa focused on the gold bangles adorning her arm. "Well, if I made it too easy, you wouldn't feel challenged."

Elias cupped her cheek. "Not challenged? With you? Never."

"I love you," Clarissa professed and pressed her forehead to his.

They indulged in another long kiss. When it ended, Elias had gone serious again.

"Have you talked to Cole?" he asked.

Clarissa was prepared to answer and then produced a tight smile instead. "Not yet."

Elias followed the line of her gaze and saw Waymon Cole just entered the gathering.

"Heard from Sophie?" Eli watched Waymon Cole mingle.

"It's been a week—a *long* week."

"These things take time."

Clarissa smiled. "I never pegged you for a patient man."

"When I want something bad enough, I can be very patient."

"Very."

"Intensely." He massaged her shoulders through the crisscross straps at the back of her petal pink gown.

She indulged in the roughly sensuous strokes from his fingers but her preoccupation only lasted a short time. Her thoughts were soon returned to Waymon Cole. It was her turn to stroke Eli's cheek then.

"I guess patience is a virtue that I don't have." She

smiled pitifully and then gathered the gown's ankle-length skirt and set off in Waymon's direction.

Elias caught her arm before she got too far.

"You can come along if you want," she offered.

Eli allowed her a bit of a head start before he whispered a curse and decided to follow.

Clarissa tracked Waymon into one of the four buffet rooms which were set up with long rectangular tables. They displayed delectables of all sorts. The room was deserted but for Waymon.

"Very generous," Clarissa noted when she entered. "This is the ten-thousand-dollar-a-plate room."

"For a good cause." Waymon shrugged and noticed Elias closing the door to the buffet room. "Come to give me the third degree?" he asked. "I thought we said all that needed to be."

Clarissa trailed her finger along the edge of a damask tablecloth. "I only want to know if my aunt died knowing that you betrayed her?"

The big fork in Waymon's hand hit the heated pan with a clatter. He kept his back turned as Clarissa moved closer.

"Or was it just knowing that the club was being taken down a shady road that did it?" she asked.

"What are you talking about?" Waymon was about to reach for the fork again but decided against it.

"I think you know exactly what I'm talking about. Jaz had so many suspicions that she went to the cops—well…the only cop she thought she could trust. She found a ledger. Did she know that it was yours, Waymon?"

"Your aunt!" Waymon suddenly snapped then.

"Humph. She didn't want to know anything." He shook his head and stared without really seeing the steaming pan of entrées.

"All of a sudden she tells me that she wants to turn her life around or some mess…make prima ballerinas out of the little wild women in that club." Waymon sneered in Clarissa's direction.

"You ungrateful bastard and this is how you repay her?"

"She should have been repaying *me!* Business boomed—some of those girls were paid insane amounts of money for private dances, weekend parties. We're one of the few clubs in this country who can fulfill our customers' *every* desire."

"Why? Because cops are bankrolling most of the fun?"

"You're damn right!" Waymon blinked when he noticed Elias again. Coming down off some of his temper, he set the plate that shook in his hand on the table.

Elias pushed himself off the door when a firm knock sounded. Outside stood the detective and two uniformed officers. At Eli's wave, they entered.

"Waymon Cole, I'm Detective Sophia Hail and we have a warrant for your arrest."

"Arrest?" Waymon spat the word. "On what charge?"

"Charges," Sophie corrected. "Which include, but aren't limited to, money laundering and racketeering." She looked over her shoulder at the crowd gathering outside the room. "Would you like for me to continue?"

"I'll be talking to your boss, Detective."

Sophie grimaced. "If you're referring to Paul Hertz, the two of you can chat in the holding cell where he's presently waiting. Although, right about now, I think he's more interested in talking to his lawyer. Read him his rights," she instructed one of the officers.

The crowd parted to make way for Waymon's shameful, handcuffed exit. He stopped just before clearing the threshold and fixed Clarissa with an unreadable look. Then he hung his head and walked away.

Sophie stopped near Clarissa. "I'm sorry that I had to do this here, but I didn't want it swept under a rug."

"Do you have enough to make it stick?" Elias asked.

"D.A. thinks so," Sophie confirmed. "With any luck, we can entice Mr. Cole to name names. Besides, our witnesses are on board."

"Witnesses?" Clarissa asked.

Sophie smiled. "Both Mr. Echols and Ms. Johnson are cooperating."

Clarissa's eyes widened. "Rena? You found her?"

"We did and she'll be fine." Sophie smiled at Eli and then back at Clarissa. "I should go."

"Sophie, thank you for working so hard to get answers to my aunt's questions."

"I couldn't have done it without help." She squeezed Clarissa's arm and winked before making her way through the talkative crowd.

Alone in the candlelit buffet room, Clarissa finally wilted and rested her head on Eli's chest.

"How are you doing?" He rubbed her arm reassuringly.

"Humph. I think this is the hardest I've ever worked for my aunt." She joined in when Eli burst into laughter.

"Do you think this is over?" she asked.

Eli kissed the top of her head. "Would you believe me if I said yes?"

Clarissa allowed her lashes to flutter dreamily. "Yes, happily," she sighed.

"And if I said I love you? Would you believe me?"

Clarissa looked up and let him see the love in her eyes. "Yes…happily." She sighed again and eagerly accepted his kiss.

Although Waymon Cole's public arrest was on everyone's lips, the Reed House Jazz Supper was a huge success. Event organizers claimed that year's dinner was its most successful yet.

Clarissa conversed with Lilia Joss. The woman was inviting her to lunch later that week and they were settling on a date when Eli arrived with Stanford Crothers.

"Sunshine!" Stan greeted Clarissa with a kiss and a quick hug. Then, he offered Lilia his arm. "If you ladies are done chattin', I'm takin' my date for a spin around this dance floor."

"They make a cute couple." Clarissa smiled when Stan whisked Lilia away.

Eli massaged the bridge of his nose. "Please don't tell Stan that."

"What?" Clarissa laughed. "You don't think there could be a wedding before the year's out?"

Elias pulled Clarissa close and they began to sway in time to the jazzy piece that piped into the room. "A wedding before the end of the year, sounds good to me," he said.

"Does it?" She propped her chin on his chest and looked up. "How good?"

Elias bent to nibble her earlobe. "As good as hearing you say you love me."

"Well, then…I love you, Elias Joss, I love you."

* * * * *

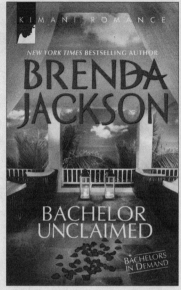

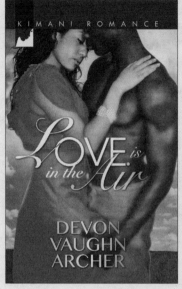

REQUEST YOUR FREE BOOKS!

2 FREE NOVELS
PLUS 2 FREE GIFTS!

KIMANI™
ROMANCE

Love's ultimate destination!